ALCHEMIST OF ETERNITY

Alchemist of Eternity

A. L. HELLAND

Willamina Studios

Contents

1

Johnson's Cabin

On the side of a mountain, half buried in the snow, was a log cabin. It was perched on a steep incline with a frozen lake below and a starry sky above. Inside were two men. One was a youth wearing thick woolen clothes, while the other was middle-aged, with a haggard, unshaven face and bloodshot eyes. This second man, Johnson, was seated on a bench beneath the window, doubled over in pain. The young man was hastily sorting through a bucket of medical supplies. He was squatting by a small oil lamp, the only light in the cabin.

Johnson was gazing out the window as he rocked back and forth, cradling his arm. "Look at the stars, Anton," he said, breaking the silence.

Anton shot him a quick glance. "Now seems hardly ze time, sir."

"Oh, Anton, you can spare a moment."

"You are losing blood, ze…"

Abruptly, Johnson's tone changed. "Anton!" he barked.

The boy dropped his jacket and stumbled across the room,

grabbing the windowsill to steady himself in the semi-darkness. "Here, sir," he said.

Johnson reached out and touched the boy's cold hand with his warm one. "I am sorry, Myshka," he said quietly, using a nickname. His hand shifted up Anton's arm and guided the boy onto the bench. "I shouldn't be so short with you."

Anton turned towards the window. It was brighter outside than in; a vast array of stars hung in the dark blue sky, casting enough light to give a dim glimmer to the river and a sparkle to distant mountains. It was a breathtaking view. But he felt a warm, sticky moisture on Johnson's arm, reminding him of his current duty. "Please, sir, may I...?" he began, looking up at the man but avoiding his eyes.

"Go ahead," Johnson said, trying to sound encouraging. "Do you know what you're doing?"

"Zere are several bad cuts and zen a compound fracture," replied Anton, a hint of doubt in his strange accent. He rose to his feet and moved the lamp onto the bench. "I will wap it up to stop ze bleeding, but first ze bone needs to be set. Closed weduction, or whatever it is called."

"Closed reduction," Johnson repeated, correcting Anton's 'r' sound. "Do you even know what that means?"

Anton knelt on the floor, looking through his limited supplies. "I zink so, sir. I zink I can set ze bone. Zen I will wap it up. We do not want it infected, sir. But why did we not go to Base? You should see a doctor."

"We're running out of equipment and personnel at Base. Besides, you're a fine enough doctor for me, Anton." Johnson looked down with a smile, and saw the slightest trace of one on the boy's face.

"I will do my best, sir." He reached for the fractured wrist. Johnson adjusted his position to give Anton a better reach of his arm. It was a bad break, right above his wrist; he knew it should not have been entrusted to a child like Anton. "Distal wadius fracture," the boy murmured, "But a compound break."

"I'm curious," said Johnson, "about how you know that. You've been mumbling about fractures and surgeries in your sleep for a while, but I've never seen you study it. Is this your newest obsession?"

"No, sir," Anton answered, pressing and prodding the wrist. "But I do know a little bit about it, I zink. I zink, sir, zat it..." he dropped his voice to a hesitant whisper. "I zink I learn it from ze Voice in my head."

Johnson tensed. "I told you to never mention the Voice again," he said, attempting to keep his voice level. "It makes no difference how quiet you whisper it."

"I am sorry, sir, but it is weally in ze head," Anton said, getting excited in the manner people do when speaking about forbidden subjects. "It is always about surgeries and medicine. It knows almost everyzing, and I zink it wants to speak wif me..."

"Enough!" Johnson grabbed the boy by the shoulders, despite the pain in his wrist. "If my bones were not broken I'd shake the living daylights out of you. Keep your mouth shut about that Voice!"

Anton went limp in his grasp, immediately humbled. Johnson released him and closed his eyes. There were a few moments of silence before the boy spoke. "I am sorry, sir. I will never do zat again. I am very, very sorry." His voice trembled. "May I see ze wist again, sir?"

Johnson held it out. He felt the boy touching it, and then heard him whisper, "Zis will not feel good, sir." And then all of a sudden pain shot up his arm and he felt a cracking, bursting sensation, like a freight train rushing across his bones. His pain tolerance hit a peak he hadn't known existed; but then the torment subsided, and he pressed his sweaty forehead against the window. Glancing down, he saw to his dismay a beam of starlight reaching through the window, gently lighting a crooked wrist and exposed bone.

"You didn't even set it," he exclaimed, his anger rising. "You didn't even do it! What did you do, try to pull it out?"

"No, sir," the boy answered, visibly shaken. "You screamed, sir. I zought I was hurting you."

"Of course it was hurting me!" Johnson shouted, sending a well-aimed kick towards the boy, partly in anger and partly to divert his mind from the lingering pain. He grasped his hand with the other and writhed in agony.

"Look at ze stars," said Anton timidly, sprawled out on his back and cradling his own wrist. "Look at zem."

Strangely enough, Johnson listened. He turned and stared out the window. There was a dash of purple above the snowy mountains, spreading towards the twinkling stars. There were so many of them; he tried to count the ones caught in a single windowpane, but it was impossible. There were far more stars here than one could ever see from Earth.

He was so enraptured by the view he hardly noticed Anton grabbing his hand again. It was only when the boy whispered, "if it hurts, hit ze window, not me," that he realized what was happening. The freight train rushed across his wrist again, but this time it rushed with more resolve. Johnson's spare hand hit the window repeatedly, and this time he realized he was screaming.

The pain level dropped, and he leaned against the window, gasping for breath. Anton wiped away the blood from the cuts and then wrapped the wrist up, using something hard as a splint that Johnson couldn't identify by touch. The window was cold, refreshingly cold for Johnson's sweating face. He turned his head slightly to put his cheek against it. With each breath he took, a frozen mist clouded the glass.

"I am finished, sir," Anton said hesitantly, unsure as to whether he would receive praise or censure.

"Thank you, Myshka." Either the stars were blinking on and off or Johnson's consciousness was drifting. A dark cloud pressed around him. He groaned and his arm ached. His stomach felt sick and there was a bad taste in his mouth, and for a moment he thought he had fainted; but then his sight returned and the stars came back. "Look at them all, Anton," he whispered. "Can you believe, there was once a time when man had never travelled through these stars. This planet was empty. This sector was uncharted." There was a rising in his stomach, but he held it back and continued. "Man could not travel in space."

"Zat was a very long time ago, sir."

"Yes, yes." Johnson looked at the boy beside him. His two diamond blue eyes reflected stars; they were set in a youthful, childish face, a face that reminded him of a man he used to know. A crop of curly hair crowned his head, again reminding Johnson of a person, this time a woman. Anton's hands were covered in blood, Johnson's blood. The man shivered.

A brisk knock at the door diverted his attention. "Open it, Myshka," he ordered, running his uninjured hand through his hair and straightening his leather jacket. Anton went to the door and admitted a broad-shouldered, grim-faced man. He had a dark, curly beard and sallow cheeks, and eyes that were unhealthily red. He greeted Johnson with a traditional bow and touch on his forehead, and then spoke to Anton in a foreign language.

The boy quickly pulled a chair across the room, placing it beside the bench. The newcomer seated himself with the dignity of a king, and then glanced at Johnson. "I have private zings to discuss wif you," he said, with an accent similar to Anton's, with the difference that he could pronounce the letter *r*.

Johnson waved Anton away. The boy gave a quick bow and touched his forehead before disappearing out the front door. The newcomer waited a few moments before speaking. "Is ze boy safely gone?"

Johnson glanced out the window. "He's in the shed," he answered. "What's your news?"

The man looked at him sideways. "I must ask about your healf, Sur Liedr."

"I'm as well as a man can be after surviving the horrors of Reka I," he growled. "And call me Johnson, Ivan. We are alone and we are friends."

Ivan nodded slowly. "Well, Johnson, let me say I am bof

surprised and impressed zat you survived Reka I. Few men do."

"Only the cowards do," Johnson answered.

"Since we are alone and we are friends," Ivan said, "Let me say zat I expected as much."

"I hung back on the expedition. I'm not risking my neck out there."

"But you are ze one who caused zis problem," Ivan reminded, "And, not zat I am bozered about zis, but you caused ze problem wif my money."

Johnson swore under his breath. "Our entire colony is on the brink of death, and all you can think about is your money? If we live through this, Ivan, I promised I would pay you back."

"After five years I find zis hard to believe."

"I'm broke, I know," Johnson said. "But once we get this force field down, I'll get the money."

Ivan pulled a pipe from his pocket and twirled it between his fingers. "I know a lot about you zat could endanger your career. Most of ze money you have spent was neizher mine nor yours. Ze Space Agency and all ze agencies back on Earf would be disgusted if zey knew a fraction of what I know."

"Look here," Johnson exclaimed, "If you're trying to threaten me..."

"I would never do a zing like zat, Sur Liedr," Ivan answered coolly. "But you are ze one wif, as we Rekans say, ze *prey position.*"

They were both quiet for a few moments. Ivan lit his pipe while Johnson cradled his wrist, and outside the sun began to rise. At length Johnson spoke. "If it's a guarantee you want, a guarantee you'll get. While I may be lacking in funds, I have treasures that could be much more to you."

"Like what?" Ivan asked, drawing at his pipe.

"Just count it as a guarantee, all right? If I can't pay you back soon enough I'll give you something that can read the future. Something that walks through time like you walk through snow. You'd know where to be and where not to be, as well as where the right investments are. That would be advantageous to you, eh? Shake on it and then tell me your news?"

"What is it?" Ivan asked, puffing away.

Johnson growled. "Well, you little blackguard, I may be using ambiguous terms but I'm not lying, not this time."

"I am not familiar wif ze English word *blackguard,*" Ivan said. "And I do not doubt zat you have such a treasure, I only doubt zat you would part wif it. When you speak of zis somezing, do you speak of ze boy?"

Johnson started. "How can you possibly know that?"

"A year ago, before all ze problems, you had a visitor from Earf. I came by to speak wif you about somefing, and zrough ze walls I overheard what your visitor said to you."

"So you're a thief, a blackmailer and an eavesdropper," Johnson exclaimed. "That must've been when Valentine came by. Blast that man, he talked loud enough to be heard from the valley. What did you hear?"

"I heard zat it is possible zat ze boy is special. But only possible," Ivan said. "It is not proven. I will take him as a guarantee, zough it is because I know he has other uses. I know you will rezink zis and try to change your mind but I will hold you to ze word, or ze blade, as my people say. Besides his imaginary power, I knew zere was somefing strange about ze boy ever since you took him in. He is not one of us."

"He was born and raised here," Johnson argued.

"Raised, yes. Born, no. Zat boy has no parents here."

"Enough about Anton," Johnson said. "I hope you had a reason for coming here other than my debt."

Ivan nodded slowly. "Madsville has radioed in. Zey have no food."

"We gave rations to all the cities," Johnson said. "They must've been careless and went through the food too quickly."

"Down at Base, we have a monf's time of food. Madsville is asking if we have any to share. What should I tell zem?"

"We did give them less than we kept," Johnson said reflectively, "And they have more people than us."

"But remember, we have got to keep ourselves alive so we can work on reducing ze force field." Ivan lowered his voice. "Some people are more important zan ozhers."

Johnson wavered and then gave in. "Tell Madsville we are out of food," he ordered.

Ivan rose to his feet and removed his pipe from his mouth. "Zat is all I came here for. I see you are injured, why are you not at ze Base?"

"After the terror of Reka I, I wanted nothing but my cabin and my mountain," Johnson answered. "But I've realized how few supplies I have here. I'll try to make my way down to the Base today to get a professional to look at this wrist."

"Zat is what you should do," Ivan agreed. "I will see you

later. In ze meantime I will send ze message to Madsville. But remember my money and your guarantee. When you have come to your senses you will regret it for I know zat you love ze boy, however you may treat him. Farewell, Sur Liedr." He bowed and left.

A few moments later, Anton came in. His cheeks and nose were red from the freezing air outside, and a few snowflakes were melting in his hair and on his woolen coat. "Is everyzing all wight, sir?" he asked, as he pulled off his boots and brushed the snow off his canvas pants.

Johnson gazed out the window, watching Ivan make his way down the steep mountain path. He clenched his teeth together. "All is well, Myshka. You should fix yourself breakfast."

"Zere is no food in ze cabin," Anton answered. "I am fine, sir, but if you are hungry I will wun to Base."

"I hope you trust that I will keep you safe," Johnson said, changing the subject abruptly.

Anton lifted his brows. "Of course, sir."

"I would never let anything happen to you," Johnson continued, watching Ivan walk out of sight.

"Zank you, sir."

"You know," he rambled, in a lightheaded tone, "It's amazing how long the stars linger in the sky after the sun has risen."

"Yes," Anton agreed, while filling up a glass of water. He came and knelt beside Johnson, handing it to him.

Johnson took it and gulped it down. His head was growing faint, and even the water didn't help much. But he had always marvelled at how the stars managed to be seen for part of the

day on this planet, and even dizziness could not quell his fascination. "You know, Anton, one of those stars is the Earth's
sun. Can you find it?"

Anton nodded and turned to the window. "It is zere, sir.
Ze dim one above ze mountain."

2

Beneath the Stars

On Earth, centuries earlier...

"Headed home, Jesse?" asked the IT director, peeking out of the computer room.

Jesse, often nicknamed Jett, stopped mid-stride and nodded. "In a minute, yes. Janet said she'd drop Logan off here, so I'm waiting for her."

"Janet's the new babysitter, isn't she?" The IT director folded his arms and leaned against the doorway, and dropped his voice to a confidential tone. "Y'know, son, I warned you about hiring a Mitchell. Their family has been known to be clueless with children." He dropped his voice even lower. "That's why there's so few of them."

Jett lifted his brows in mock surprise. "How could you speak of your own cousins like that?"

The director shook his head. "I know them, that's all."

"I'll see you around, uncle," Jett said, striding off. He was a sworn officer there in the Justice Center of Angel, Nebraska. The IT director, who worked in adjoining rooms, was related to him, as was nearly everyone in Angel, which was a miniscule town where it was hard to find someone who was not your cousin. Jett turned a corner and nearly collided with a woman holding a baby.

"Pardon me," he said, stepping back. The lobby had several mothers, one or two fathers, and a handful of children, all of whom were listening to one of the volunteer officers who was giving a tour. She had asked for questions, and five of the kids were holding up their hands excitedly. Jett stopped to listen.

"Do you ever catch badguys?" the first one asked.

After all five had asked their questions, it was clear they were only interested in the image of a cop chasing a robber. Jett smiled and shook his head and moved on. As he neared the desk he was aiming for, he was interrupted by a sudden grab on his shirt collar.

"Hold up, Teddy, don't choke me," he said, knowing instantly who it was. Teddy had a habit of seizing him by the collar whenever he got excited, which was fairly often. This was the third time that day.

"Quick, I need your help!" Teddy panted, pulling harder. "I'm in so much trouble. I've got them stuck, and it's broke, and…"

"What did you do?"

"It wasn't just me," he said defensively. "It's your fault, too. It's the new lock we put on the back door of the patrol car. I was showing it to a couple of families on the tour, you know, and it started… not working right. Can you fix it? Please?"

Jett gently but firmly removed his friend's hand. "Of course. Let's go take a look."

"Yes, and hurry!" Teddy said.

Together they dashed down the hallway, which was choked with the families Jett had seen in the lobby a few moments before. The two young men jostled their way through the crowd (with an occasional "pardon me, cousin Sarah,") and then punched in the security code for the back door. Outside, the immediate area behind the Justice Center was concrete, with an overhanging roof supported by pillars. Several of their patrol cars were parked here, and one in particular was surrounded by a few wide-eyed children and their parents. Jett's presence had a calming effect on them; he was a small man, with a calm, unassuming face and character that inspired trust in the people he dealt with. He stepped up to the patrol car and tried the door.

"It won't open, see?" Teddy said, leaning over his shoulder and breathing down his neck. He was taller than Jett, who was rather on the short side.

Teddy usually used this car. The back seat was secured with bars dividing it from the front seat and over the windows, designed for bringing in difficult customers. Usually it opened with a key; but after Teddy had lost the key, he and Jett, always looking for something new to invent, had put in a fingerprint sensor and connected it with the lock. The idea was that when either of them touched the handle it would unlock, but not for anyone else. They had been wild with their success and were still trying to convince their higher-ups that it was a brilliant alteration.

"I kept putting my finger on it, Jett," Teddy explained. He had tousled, dirty blond hair, brown eyes, and a strong tendency for trouble. "It won't do anything. Oh, and I had let a few kids try it out."

"Try out the backseat?" Jett spluttered, smashing his nose against the window. Sure enough, two frightened five-year olds were staring back at him.

"What do we do if we can't get it unlocked?" Teddy whimpered.

"Shhh." Jett carefully placed his finger on and off the sensor pad, listening for the click of the lock. But nothing happened.

Teddy was still whining over his shoulder. "We've been on a record of *not* getting in trouble for such a long time. You have, at any rate. I guess me on the other hand..."

Ignoring him, Jett knelt and pried off the sensor pad. Reaching his hand into the cavity behind the handle, he fumbled about for a moment before finding the right spot. He jerked out a wire.

"I heard it unlock!" cried a woman who Jett vaguely knew as a distant cousin, and who was obviously one of the mothers. She jerked open the door, unknowingly hitting Jett in the head with it and sending him sprawling.

Teddy extended his hand and pulled his friend up. He seemed slightly flustered. "You disconnected our fingerprint sensor. It was very handy. Get it? Handy? We unlock it with our hands, our fingers? ... Never mind. But I liked that sensor. It saved a lot of time."

"That's the third time I had to remove the handle to unlock the door," Jett scolded. "You'd better find the key. This invention is useless, anyway. If you and I ever make a new one we'll have to change a few things, like the fact that any criminal could pry it off as easily as I just did."

"Jesse!" they heard a woman call. It was Janet, the babysitter. She was a woman in her mid-thirties, and she held the hand of a young boy. "There you are, Jesse. Logan was a very good boy today. We did a little school, and then he drew a picture for you. He set it down in the office while we were looking for you."

"Thank you, Janet," Jett said, shaking her hand. He sank to his knees to be at eye-level with his son. "Would you like to show it to me right away?"

The six-year-old nodded. "Sure, Daddy."

"He spent a lot of time on it," Janet chattered as she handed him a bag full of Logan's snacks and crayons. "You have a very detail-oriented son. I assume you've got him from here. Enjoy your time with him, and I'll see you Sunday."

"Thank you again, Janet. See you Sunday."

Janet disappeared and Jett slung the bag over his shoulder. Teddy grinned at him. "Look at this fine specimen of a father. A model boy at his side, a purse on his arm…"

"Teddy, I want you to find that key before you leave this station today," Jett said seriously. "Do you hear me?"

"Look here, it wasn't my fault," Teddy began, but a look from his friend cut him short. "All right, I'm sorry. I'll find it." He sighed, and then his voice turned dreamy. "You know, we should try our hands at higher things. I give up on revolutionizing this station. Remember the inventions we used to make with Maddie before she…?"

"No." For a fleeting moment, Jett was reminded of his wife Maddie, who had been a beautiful woman with stars in her eyes and stars in her mind. Maddie, Teddy and he had spent years on inventions that were far more grand than the dull things Jett came up with around the station. They had wanted to reach the stars. But Maddie had been gone nearly four years, and with her had gone all his desire to invent with such lofty goals.

Teddy sighed again. "I'm sorry, Jett. But we were going to build ships and go to space, remember? But here we are, still in Nebraska, giving out parking tickets and watching crosswalks!"

"You can still go to the stars, and I'm sure you will. Just don't bring me with you." He began walking toward the door with his steady, even stride. He noticed little Logan, pushing himself to keep up with his father, was beginning to imitate the way he walked. They stepped inside the building and Jett shut the door behind them.

The little boy looked up at him. "Can I use the bathroom?" he asked. His eyes were glossy with tears.

Jett felt a surge of panic. He could face all the grim realities of being a police officer, but he was helpless when faced with a crying child. "Of course, son. I'll be in the office," he said, faking cheerfulness, which he hoped would help. Logan disappeared down the hallway. He was very sensitive, and there was no knowing what had bothered him this time. Jett knew that it must be a downside to not having a mother.

He walked into the office and sank into a swivel chair. His gaze landed on a sheet of dark blue paper, covered with white crayon and pieces of construction paper that had been glued on and were not yet dry. He squinted and angled his head, trying to decipher what the round bulb in the middle was supposed to be. Suddenly the picture became clear. It was a space helmet.

It was Logan's picture, featuring a happy-looking astronaut beside a circle of gray construction paper, which was either supposed to be a moon or a meteorite. The stars were etched out with white crayon, which was also used for the inscription at the bottom. In Logan's childish but concise hand was written *My Daddy*. Jett's breath caught as he read it.

Even Logan knew the fascination his father had once held toward the stars. Jett hovered over the picture for a moment, unsure as to whether he should rip it or hang it on the wall. Deciding on neither, he left it lying where it was.

He met Logan outside the bathroom and the two headed home in silence. Jett King lived there in Angel, in a little house on a quiet road. Inside, the main room had a worndown easy-chair and a couch that had been barely used at all. One of the lights in the three-bulb fixture was flickering and the other two were dead. A family picture hung on the wall. It was four years old, and had dark-haired Jett, pretending to smile, and Maddie, curly-haired and beaming, though they had both known at that time that she was dying. She held two-year-old Logan in her lap while Jett held a baby. Nowadays, Jett hardly noticed the picture.

He rummaged through the refrigerator and found leftover oatmeal for Logan to eat. He didn't fix himself any, as he and Teddy had planned to eat dinner together late that night, after Teddy got off work. When Logan was finished Jett helped him into his pajamas. After this, the two of them got into the car again and drove twenty minutes to the neighboring town, where Jett bought the cheapest Chinese food he could find, which he personally despised but knew that Teddy loved. They drove home and then Jett tucked his son into bed.

Settling down in his easy chair, Jett picked up a book. It was written by a lieutenant during World War II, who had been stationed somewhere in the South Pacific and had helped with stopping Japanese supply ships from reaching their bases. He dozed off a few times, and then finally put the book down and got up to fix himself tea. He sat down again, and his foot began to tap in even rhythm with the old clock on the mantel.

Suddenly his phone rang. He fumbled for his pocket and pulled it out. "Hello? Jesse King."

"Hey, Jett, it's Ted," came the familiar voice. "Sorry, but I can't come."

"I've been sitting here for an hour waiting," Jett complained. "Why not?"

Jett could hear the shrug in his voice. "I'm tired, that's all."

Jett glanced at the Chinese food on the coffee table. "You can't just change your mind an hour after you're supposed to show up. Have you been avoiding me? It seems like Logan and I only see you at work these days."

"I'm sorry, I really am."

"Do you want me to come over there?" Jett asked. "I just put Logan to bed, but we can come by tomorrow. Things never turn out well when you hole yourself up in that old house of yours."

"No! No, don't come over here," Teddy said. "I'm beyond exhausted, I'll probably sleep half the day tomorrow. Goodnight."

"Goodnight," Jett sighed.

He hung up and slouched in his chair, glaring at the un-eaten Chinese food.

3

Time-Travel

Jett had gotten up to put the food into the fridge when a knock at the door interrupted him. He had been sitting in his chair for a while after the phone call, and Teddy lived only a few minutes away, so at first he imagined his friend had changed his mind. Replacing the food on the coffee table, he hurried over and opened the door. But he had been wrong to hope; standing in his doorway was a stranger, his eyes fixed on the ground.

"Are you Jesse King?" the stranger asked before Jett could shut the door. He was surprised to hear his name.

"Yes, I am. What can I do for you, sir?"

"You have a son named Logan?"

"... Yes."

"And a deceased wife, Maddie?"

Jett felt himself wince. "Yes."

"I have urgent business to discuss with you. Can I come in please?"

Jett tilted his head. "Who are you?"

"It would be better if I explained inside."

Jett opened the door a little wider, not entirely sure why. The stranger stepped in and seated himself on the couch. He had the agile frame of a twenty-year-old and a headful of chestnut hair, but he hung his head with the weight of an old man. Closing the door, Jett settled into his easy chair again.

"I'm very sorry," the stranger began, his eyes fixed on his lap. "I'm afraid I have to change your life. It will never really be the same again. Everything that you think is impossible will happen before your very eyes. Is that Chinese I smell?"

Jett nodded, unable to speak.

The stranger shook his head sadly. "Nasty stuff."

"Who are you?" Jett managed to say. He kept his face expressionless as usual, but it was not hard to tell by his darting eyes that his mind was racing.

"My name is Duke," the stranger said, his face still turned downwards. "And I've come because my team has picked up some disturbance around you."

Jett's eyebrows arched. "Are you some sort of agent?"

"Not exactly. We've found time-disturbance."

Jett blinked. "What?"

"Do you believe time-travel is possible, Mr. King?"

"No," Jett said bluntly. "My friend Teddy does, so I've heard all about it. It was one of the things he and Maddie were obsessed with."

"Time-travel has been done before," Duke said. "In a linear timeline, it was accomplished for the first time four years ago, here in the unimportant town of Angel. It's been done several times since then."

"I think it's time you go home," Jett said.

Duke put his face in his hands. "I wish I didn't have to be the person to convince you of this."

"Time-travel, so what, big deal!" Jett shrugged, following the same instincts he did when Logan was about to cry. "Even if it is possible, why are you here? I didn't do it, if that's what you're wondering."

"Mr. King, I am about to ask you some very tough questions. Where is your son?"

"Logan is in bed. But I don't want him coming down to hear any of this mumbo jumbo." He lifted his cold tea and took a sip.

"No, not Logan. Where is your other son?"

Jett spit out his mouthful. "Other son? I don't have one. Before my wife died, she had a weak little thing, but it didn't live long. Neither of them did."

"How, exactly, did your wife die?"

"What right do you have to ask me that?"

"Forgive me. But how did your son die, the baby? Can't you remember?"

"Why does it matter?"

"Mr. King," the man said softly, "The first time that time-travel happened was when your second son was three weeks old. It happened days before your wife and baby died. We've detected a paradox surrounding you during that time. We want to know what happened."

"I don't know what you're talking about!" Jett exclaimed.

Duke reached forward and picked up one of the boxes of food on the coffee table. He turned it around in his hands, studying it; there was almost a surreal glow to his hands, a glow of fire and gold. Jett, who had watched Teddy practice sleight-of-hand tricks for many years, watched carefully, but try as he might he could not detect the man doing anything with it other than hold it. "If you were to find a message written inside this box," Duke said, handing it over, "What would you want it to say?"

"Perhaps something along the lines of *you are kind and hospitable*," Jett said. "The people I let into my house…"

Without thinking of what he was doing, he opened it. And there, above the cold food, was a message written with pencil in elegantly sharp handwriting that made him think of flames and ash. His eyes widened as he read the words: *You are kind and hospitable.*

"Did it work?" Duke asked, his voice more grating than it had been before.

"What did you do?" asked Jett, astonished.

"I haven't done it yet," Duke answered. His breathing was suddenly heavy, like a man after a race. "I'll go back in time and write it in before they hand it to you. If it worked then that means I'll manage it."

Jett looked at him skeptically. "Not every time-traveller would be able to do that. You changed the *present* by *thinking* about what you will do in the *past*, though you haven't done it yet."

"You're a sharp man, Mr. King." For the first time, Duke lifted his head. Jett started. Duke's eyes, which had remained hidden until this time, were alive. They flickered like burning coals, tossing and rolling. His eyes were not brown or blue or green, but orange; they were orbs of fire with dark pupils in the middle.

"It's rather complicated," Duke began, his eyes dimming with apology. "My time-travel energy allows me to control things, sometimes. I generally have a clear sense of what I can do and what I can't. I'm a time-traveller, in a way, that is. I'm a creation, fabrication, of time; I can feel it and I can see it. But perhaps I can explain it later. For now we need to speak about your son."

"Let's assume I believe all this," Jett said. "What about my son?"

"We must find him," Duke said. "I believe he may have been stranded in another time-period."

A flame of hope kindled in Jett's heart. Even though his mind urged him not to, he found himself believing for a moment that it could all be true. "Maddie!" he exclaimed. "My wife, could she..."

Duke shook his head. "Maddie is dead. Everything you remember about her is correct. But as for your son, we found a temporal paradox dating to the time of his disappearance. I believe that somebody purposely confused your memories of him to make you believe he had died."

"Who would do that?"

"There are only three people who could've caused the displacement: you, Maddie, or Teddy Johnson."

Jett experienced a nauseous feeling that could only be compared with being punched in the stomach. If, *if* that was true, then his life truly never would be the same. He wished that Angel was smaller, that he was smaller, that nobody could see him and he could hide in a corner with no pressure and no accountability. Nothing he had heard that night had been pleasant. He grasped his jet-black hair and pulled until the tears came, but he was still in his easy-chair and he still had to find something to say.

"Please, Mr. King," Duke spoke again. "Could you visit my office tomorrow? There we can give you full details of what happened, and what we intend to do. It's my duty to repair time, and I believe it's yours to find your son."

"I...I... Give me the address, and I'll be there," Jett managed to say. "I want to know how much of this is the truth."

"So you believe that some of it may be true?"

"Of course," Jett said. "With Teddy, anything is possible."

Duke left his office address and then left without another word. Jett was left alone with his thoughts. Man suffers more in his imagination than in reality, as the philosopher has said, yet both reality and imagination tormented him as he struggled through the night. Time-travel was real; or at least it was real enough that a man had come to tell him about it, and the man had had fire in his eyes. Jett tossed and turned in his easy-chair before trying his bed. There he had a vivid dream about Maddie and Teddy displacing a baby through time, and the family picture on the wall which he had nearly forgotten played a prominent role.

The following morning he found himself in Angel's center. Though the town was small it was bustling and full of business that sustained their economy, as well as helping those of neighboring, larger towns. The Mitchells, Kings, Emmetts, and other various family branches were entrepreneurs. The card Duke had left brought him to a tall, brick-faced building that he had seen countless times but had never paid attention to. Stepping inside, he found a lobby with signs on the wall. They explained which floor had what offices.

It was the cheapest place to rent a room and Jett could see why. There were cracks in the floor and ceiling, as if the building had been trying to stretch and had almost fallen apart. The halls had a mingled smell of disinfectant and infected things. He hurried onto the second floor and searched for the right room, at last finding it at a door with the number *16*. He hesitated, but then he squared his shoulders and knocked.

The door opened. It was a small, square room, with mostly computers of all shapes and sizes. A young lady was typing at a desk, her blond hair in a messy bun, while an older man stood by the printer. It was Duke who had opened the door. "Good morning, Mr. King," he greeted. "Thank you for meeting with me today." His eyes were balls of fire, just like the day before, so Jett concluded that they must be a permanent thing. But he did notice that the flames were lesser and softer than they had previously been.

Jett stepped in cautiously. He was wearing jeans and a North Face jacket, his usual outfit when not at work. Today he was supposed to be fishing with Logan, but instead he had asked Janet Mitchell to babysit him, and while she had agreed, she had not done so in the best of grace. Jett hoped he would be able to get to the bottom of this time-travel business quickly, but he had the feeling that time-travel didn't work that way.

"Jesse King, everybody," Duke announced to the other two people in the room. "Mr. King, this is Parker Quinn," he waved at the girl at the desk who smiled, "and this is Dr. Emmett."

"Dr. Emmett!" Jett said in surprise, noticing him for the first time. The doctor was his uncle, a man of medium height with a wise, kind face. He had thick, dark hair and beard that was turning white around his ears.

"Good morning, Jesse," Dr. Emmett said. "How are you?"

"Good, I suppose. So, you know..." he glanced at Duke. "I mean, why are you here?"

"I've known Duke for a long time," the doctor answered. "I know what you're thinking, son, and yes. Time-travel is a secret I've known about for a while. I often wondered why Duke was here in Nebraska, but I guess this whole time he's been looking for you." He turned back to the computer where the young woman was sitting. "On a different note, what's this report you're having her write up, Duke? Why's it about Tate?"

Duke joined him in looking over the girl's shoulder. "It's all right, isn't it?" Parker asked, brushing a strand of hair from her face. "I've got the dates you wanted, the names, addresses..."

"Yes, it's perfect," Duke said. "Emmett, this is about my investigation. I believe Thomas O. Emmett, or Tate as you call him, has been the victim of temporal displacement."

"Who's Tate Emmett?" asked Jett.

"He's a boy my sister adopted as a baby," Dr. Emmett said. "You've probably seen him here and there. I've always been like a father to him. How did he get mixed up in this mess, Duke? You can't possibly be saying he has anything to do with time-travel."

"I'm afraid Mr. King holds the answer to our questions, whether he realizes it or not," Duke answered.

Jett was growing tired of being called Mr. King. "Look, sir, my babysitter wasn't planning on watching Logan today. I've got to pick him up by noon. If we could get to the point..."

"Certainly, sorry," Duke said, leaning against Parker's desk. "Could you take us to Teddy Johnson?"

Some inner sense warned Jett that something was about to change forever. Fighting against this thought, he said, "Teddy can't be involved in any of your... your... conspiracy theories. He couldn't have done anything."

"I'm afraid he did something," Duke said. "Two hundred years from now, do you know who is credited with discovering time-travel?"

"Of course we don't know, Duke," Dr. Emmett pointed out

"Well, it's a man named Teddy Johnson," Duke said. "I've been doing research on him, but there isn't much out there. He was born in this town, and lived in this town. After demonstrating his time-travelling invention, he disappeared and was never proven to have been seen again."

Concern flitted across Jett's face. "What? When does he disappear?"

Duke glanced at his large, square watch. "Today."

For a moment Jett could not breathe and he could not think. The idea was preposterous... far-fetched... insane! Not time-travel itself; he had sat up through the night many times listening to Maddie and Teddy's ideas, and they had seemed feasible. It was possible, perhaps. But as for his son still being alive, kidnapped or displaced into time somewhere, or his best friend Teddy about to disappear forever?

Thunk. The door hit Jett in the back of the head and he crumpled to the floor, stars spinning in his eyes.

"Oh... sorry," said the intruder, still holding the door and gaping down at Jett. "Didn't know you were there."

"Robbie, you are always pushing and slamming things with unnecessary force," Parker scolded. "Slow down and stop rushing about!"

Realizing that nobody was planning on helping him up, Jett pulled himself to his feet. He glanced over at Robbie. The man was several inches taller than him, and definitely younger. He had a mop of thick, wheat-blond hair; he wore sturdy brown boots and a brown shirt. His pants were covered with mysterious dark splotches that smelled like diesel fuel, and matched the stains on the rag he held.

"You must be Jesse King," he said, holding out a greasy hand. "I'm Robert Juno Finley, and very happy to meet you."

Jett glanced from the man's broad, childish smile to his stained hand. Cautiously he extended his own. Robert Juno Finley grabbed it and shook it heartily.

"You can call me Robbie," the young man continued, as Jett wiped his hand on his jacket. "I'm a pilot, or at least I try."

"And what do you pilot?"

Robbie grinned. "The finest ship you'll ever meet. A 3000 special edition model, a wonder for her day. Pointed and sleek, with those funny little green lights on her tail. She flies like a charm. It was after I watched her beat the *Starlight 2990* that I..." he stopped abruptly and coughed. "I took her."

"He's talking about a spaceship that he stole," Dr. Emmett clarified, folding his arms.

"The *Starlight 3000*," Robbie said. "And I didn't steal it. Now that we have Jesse King, we can clear up the mystery and catch the real thief!" he turned to Jett in excitement. "Maybe you can explain what that Johnson scoundrel was up to!"

"I don't know what you're talking about," Jett said.

Duke intervened. "Might you have a picture of Johnson with you?"

"On my phone, sure," Jett said.

"May I see it?"

Jett pulled out his phone and handed it over. Duke pressed a couple of buttons, and then held it up so everyone could see the screen. It was a picture Jett's mother had taken for him, during a picnic at the creek. It featured messy-haired Teddy, little Logan, and Jett, each holding the crawdads they had caught.

"That's him!" Robbie exclaimed. "He was a lot older when I saw him, though. That's the scoundrel who zapped me out of orbit and time!"

4

The Paradox

A short while later, Jett found himself in his car driving to Teddy's house. Duke was following behind in a car of his own. Jett was unsure as to whether it was wise to lead this stranger to his friend's home, and he was plagued with doubts and misgivings over the five minutes it took to reach it. It was an old house with two stories that had undoubtedly looked cozy once upon a time, but not anymore. The garden was overgrown. Weeds and thistles covered the lawn and arbor. The paint on the house was chipped and peeling, while the porch was rotten and hardly strong enough to bear a man's weight.

The house had once belonged to Teddy's parents, but they had passed away several years before. Jett had never understood how his friend could continue to live here. The place was in terrible disrepair, and it felt like dead people.

He stepped out of his car and glanced at Duke, who had just walked up. Jett immediately noticed something different about the man, as if he had been transformed into an entirely different person within minutes. His eyes were rolling with a rage Jett could not understand, while he stood stiff and erect, like a bloodhound on a strong scent. The mild, apologetic man was gone, replaced with a wounded and wrathful creature.

For a moment Jett hesitated, but then summoning his courage he walked past the porch towards the garage door. "He's probably in here. Teddy always works on his inventions on Saturdays."

Duke followed him silently.

"Teddy?" Jett opened the garage door. The wall immediately to his right was covered with charts and graphs, some related to science, some to economy, and some just to Teddy's random musings. Years ago, Jett had helped to make a few. On the floor were special replica space helmets, their shiny whiteness and value contrasting sharply with a thick layer of cobwebs and dust.

Teddy was there. He was in the middle of the garage, rummaging through a backpack. An elaborate array of wires was spread about his feet.

"Jett!" Teddy jumped in surprise, hiding the backpack behind him. "I wasn't expecting you!"

"What are you doing? What's all this stuff?"

"He's setting up a field displacer and a vortex manipulator," Duke said after one glance.

Jett blinked. "What?"

"He's time-travelling," Duke clarified. His voice was unfamiliar and stern.

Teddy turned his starry eyes to Jett. "It's possible," he breathed. "It really is. I meant to tell you, I really did!"

"How could you keep something like this from me?" Jett

asked. He could feel his cozy sense of reality crumbling about him. "How many times have you done it?"

"Only a few times! It's unimaginable, Jett, beyond your wildest dreams. With power like this, we could turn history itself into our own goldmine!"

"Johnson!" Duke interrupted. "What did you do to Mr. King's son?"

A lump lodged itself in Jett's throat. His best friend could not have done anything, not innocent Teddy.

But an unnatural fear was flickering in the young man's eyes. "I... I didn't do anything..."

"Don't lie to me," Duke said hotly. "You've cut a hole through time, and I can feel it."

"I didn't mean to," Teddy whimpered. "It was years ago, right before Maddie died. Jett, you were telling me about how she needed most of the day to rest, so you were watching Logan and the baby for her."

Jett vaguely remembered that type of conversation. That part of his life had been a blur he didn't want to remember.

"You mentioned, Jett, that you found the baby crying at noon. Noon."

Noon? Jett could not see the significance.

"I went home and tried my time-machine for the first time," Teddy continued in his pathetic whimper. "I figured that I wouldn't try putting myself too far ahead or behind, since it was my first time. I set it for the day before, right before noon. I wanted to watch you through the window when you found the baby crying."

"And it worked?" Duke pushed.

"Yes, it did! I was in my garage still, but it was the day

before, all over again! I could hear myself singing upstairs! I hurried out and ran to Jett's house, and found the window to the bedroom. I wanted to watch what he did so I could astound him with details when I got back to my regular time. The window was ground level, and open. The baby was crying."

He moistened his dry lips with his tongue. "I couldn't bear to hear the baby crying. Jett was taking too long to come, so I... I climbed in and picked him up."

Jett's eyebrows shot up.

"I wondered what would happen if I changed the past. An experiment! There's so much we could do for mankind if we were able to change history. So I thought, start with a little experiment. I took the baby with me and..."

"My *son* was your little experiment?" Jett exclaimed, crossing the room in one stride. He grasped his friend by the collar, like Teddy was always doing to him, albeit much more seriously. "You must have killed him, or erased him from existence or something!"

"I didn't!" Teddy protested. "I would *never* let anything happen to any of your sons, Jesse. I took the baby back to my regular time. I kept my hands on him the whole time, I swear. I went over to your house and left him in the car for a minute. I was planning on asking you what had happened that day, since I had changed history. I thought your story would change, and you would say you weren't able to find your baby. I was going to give him straight back safe and sound, I swear."

"Time is not something to be trifled with," Duke said.

"You created a paradox. Time fights against that to protect itself."

"That must've been what it did," Teddy said, cowering. Jett's hands were still by his throat. "Your story didn't change, Jett. You let me inside and there, there was the baby!"

Duke's eyes flamed, while Jett's breath caught in his throat. "There was one in your car, and one in my house," he croaked.

"Exactly, Jett. Two babies when there should have been one. I didn't know what to do! My time-travel was supposed to be a great feat... I would tell you the story in triumph... we'd learn how to properly manipulate time for good! But you wouldn't listen to me if you heard what I did to your son. And then Maddie died that week..." He swallowed, and Jett relaxed his grip on him. "You couldn't handle anything. I put both of the babies in different homes and we reported that they died. I went through so much trouble to bury a baby that wasn't dead, but everyone believed the lie."

Jett let go of Teddy completely. "Does this mean I have two sons, one of them impossibly real, floating around time somewhere?"

Teddy cringed. "Yes. I can find them for you."

"No you won't," Duke said. "You'll let me know where to look, and I'll find them. I'm putting you under arrest. Where I come from, the 23rd century, you're wanted for several crimes. And besides that, I can't allow you to manipulate time-travel like this."

"Forget it!" Teddy laughed, almost manically. "Look here, I *invented* time-travel! I can do what I like with it! And imagine what we could do," he turned to Jett. "We could stop so many people from ever dying in the past. We'd give humanity a brighter history to be proud of."

"Teddy, I..." started Jett, but his friend interrupted.

"And we'd see the future! With time-travel, we could bounce around from time to time, taking what we need, amassing supplies and friends it would normally take years to build up, but we could live years in days! And relive the best moments! They reach planets in the future, Jett, *planets*! Liveable, breathable ones. We could craft a civilization on one with years of history, all in a day! With time-travel, we make the rules."

The stars were back in his eyes. He grasped Jett's shoulders. "I invented it. It's my domain. And nobody can take it from us, and they can't blame us, either. We could bring Maddie back. We'd zap into the future and find a cure for her sickness. You could bring it to her. Walk into that hospital room, sit on the edge of that cursed bed, and tell her you've pulled time and space apart to save her!"

"Stop!" Duke ripped the two apart. "Jett, you can't listen to him. He's under investigation for several crimes. Attempted robbery of a spacecraft, political crimes and scandals, forgery, murder of a..."

"No," Teddy breathed. "I would never do that." Picking up his backpack, he slung it over his shoulder and then pressed a button on the floor with his foot. "You missed this chance, Jett. I'll come back for you."

"Teddy, you can't leave!"

"Look to the stars," he said, and winked.

Suddenly he was gone.

Duke staggered back as if in pain, while Jett stood frozen to the spot. Before he could think, he felt a rush of air on his face. Stars shimmered where Teddy had disappeared and then formed into a figure. One last gust and Teddy Johnson was standing before them once again. But with one glance, Jett's stomach dropped and he was more horrified than he had ever been in his life.

It was Teddy Johnson, yes, but he was different. His hairline had receded, and his dirty-blond hair was thinning and had turned brown. He seemed broader, his arms were thicker, and in general his boyish frame was now developed into a man's. An entirely different outfit encased him: steel-toed boots, thick canvas pants, and a leather jacket. A large, square-faced watch hung on his arm. His youthful exuberance had been wiped off his face, replaced by the quiet look of a tired man.

At least his voice had not changed. "What the..." he glanced back and forth from Jett to Duke, and then ended in a curse (his language had certainly changed).

"Teddy!" Jett screeched. "Are you fifty?"

The man glared. "Thirty-eight," he said.

Duke was hunched over and breathing heavily, but the fire in his eyes was tossing and turning. "Why did you come back here?"

"I found this time coordinate in my old notebook, so I decided to follow it to grab a few mementos. I forgot that it would bring me here. Look here, Jesse King, it's been a while, for me, anyway, and I have loads that I should tell you. There is so much out there. You should've come. I had almost forgotten this day… I offered you a chance."

"You've spent over a decade somewhere else," Jett said, attempting to wrap his mind around it.

"And I accomplished the work of a millenium! The stars, Jesse, the planets! They have it all, in the future. Do you remember when I went on about the opportunities we had?"

"It was only a minute ago!"

"Ah yes." Teddy closed his eyes. "Jesse, it is a life worth living. Every day I spend where I want. When you live linear, from day to day, you've got to wade through the bad times when you want to have a good time. Not with time-travel. There's no real accountability, Jesse. I answer to no one!"

Duke laid a hand on the man's shoulder. "The crimes, Johnson. My city, Simul Atlantis, sent me to find you. Now that some time has passed, I'm sure you know what I mean."

From the look on Teddy Johnson's face, he certainly did. Duke led him out of the garage.

Jett climbed onto a shelf where Teddy kept his yard tools. Up on the highest shelf was a rusty pickaxe. Grabbing it, he jumped down with a yell and attacked Teddy's invention that he had first used to time-travel. Every wire he tore apart. Every button he cracked and smashed out of its casing. He then turned and struck the maps off the walls, put dents into the space helmets, and with a final yell imbedded the pickaxe into the wall of Teddy's old house. He sank to his knees.

Of all the impossible things! His best friend, aged fourteen years in seconds. His dead son, alive and split into two. A chance to save Maddie, a chance he had just destroyed. He didn't understand it, and wouldn't understand it until much later, but he didn't feel any guilt.

Leaving the pickaxe in the wall, he walked outside. To his surprise, he found only Duke and Robbie. He had known that Robbie had come in the car with Duke, and had wondered why he had never come out. But what surprised him most was the absence of Teddy Johnson.

"What happened?" he demanded. "Where did Teddy go?"

"His watch was a portable vortex manipulator," Duke answered. The gleam in his eyes was fading, and the former, milder man was returning. "I knew before I came that if Johnson could time-travel, it was a certain means of escape for him if I could not find his manipulator quickly enough. That's why I brought Robbie; he and I have been working on some equipment to track down time-displacement. But I'm not sure he scanned the area quickly enough."

"Begging your pardon," huffed Robbie, glancing over, "The moment Johnson beamed away I was here on the spot. I scanned it as fast as I could."

"So he's gone," Jett said. "Teddy is gone." He felt strangely weak.

"Yes," Duke said. "But it might please you to hear that we have found your son... one of them, at any rate. Dr. Emmett's nephew, Thomas Emmett, the adopted son of the doctor's sister. I'm told they call him Tate."

At the very idea of his newfound son, Jett swooned. He didn't want a real, tangible example of how his life was changed forever. He grasped the door to support himself from the pressing darkness, wondering if pure shock could make a person as sick as he felt. Maybe he was insane, he thought, and the idea actually brought him comfort. He pushed his head against the door, but then immediately regretted it as pain richoted behind his forehead. He slumped onto the floor and saw a swirl of stars, and then everything went black.

5

Thomas Emmett

The next thing Jett knew, he was lying on a saggy couch with a bag of ice stuffed under his head. He groaned and sat up. There was a TV sitting on a shelf to his right, a carpet on the floor, a newspaper on the coffee table, and a basket of flowers by a sliding glass back door. It was a normal living room, far too normal, he thought, for the nightmare he had found himself in.

"Jesse, is your head all right?" spoke a girl's voice. Jett jumped and blinked the last few floaties from his eyes before turning to see who it was. It was Parker Quinn, the blond girl he had seen in Duke's office. She was sitting on a chair beside him.

"Yes, I think so." He rubbed his forehead and then squeezed the bridge of his nose, trying to fight back the headache.

"Here, sip some water," a new voice said, startling him. Somebody pushed a glass into his hands.

Jett turned to look at this new person. It was a teenage boy, perhaps sixteen or seventeen. He had short, cropped hair, diamond blue eyes, and an air of competence. He was built small; he was shorter than Parker Quinn, who was no taller than average for women. He smiled as he saw Jett scanning him over.

"My name's Tate Emmett," he said. "Drink your water."

Jett's eyes rolled back and he went limp. For a moment he saw stars again. The water sloshed around, but before the cup could fall from his hands, Tate had grabbed and steadied his arm. His other hand supported Jett's head, giving him a quick shake and keeping him sitting up.

The water in the cup steadied. "Quick save," Jett muttered, the swoon passing as quickly as it had come.

"I know when a patient is blacking out," said Tate. "Keep yourself together. Your head will stop spinning in a minute."

If the past day was anything to go by, Jett imagined that his head would not stop spinning for a while yet.

"So you're Tate," Jett said, wondering who had named this boy. He could think of dozens of names he liked better. "Thomas Emmett, right?" He strained his memory, wondering if he had seen this boy at any family reunions, but his face was unfamiliar.

"Yes sir," Tate answered, "the same. And you are Jesse King."

Jett tilted his head and looked at Tate's eyes. They were diamond blue, a vivid copy of Maddie's. He searched for some trace of nervousness, or shock, in the boy's expression. He wanted to know if he knew.

Tate stared back unflinchingly. It was difficult to decipher what that look meant.

"Look," he said, sitting up so the boy could stop supporting him, "could you leave us alone for a moment? I'd like to speak with Parker Quinn... privately."

"Of course. Drink your water, sir."

Thomas disappeared. Setting the glass on the coffee table, Jett turned desperate eyes to the young blond woman. "Is that really... I mean, do you know if..."

"That is Tate, your son," she answered. "And please, call me either Parker or Quinn. It's getting annoying, hearing both of them at once. Personally I don't even think they sound good together."

"Which do you prefer? Parker or Quinn?"

She shrugged. "Duke calls me Park, they call me Quinn at school, and Cariss calls me sweetie. It doesn't make much difference to me as long as it's short."

Jett wasn't going to be calling her sweetie, so that narrowed down the choices.

"Parker, does Tate know who I am?" he asked.

She nodded. "Yes, he does. We've spent the past hour explaining it to him."

He started. "I've been out for an hour? I just got a little surprised and hit my head against the wall!"

"You've been under enormous stress," she retorted. "Duke told me what happened in Johnson's garage. It must have been a trying ordeal."

"Johnson... I mean Teddy... are they tracking him down?"

"Yes," she answered. "We can easily trace time-distortion with Duke's watch. Robbie's been working on it."

"But do you have to? You should leave him alone," he pleaded.

Her eyebrows arched slightly. "Duke has a mission to protect time, which in turn protects innocent people. Time-travel may not be wrong, but that doesn't justify its every use, just like any other kind of tool. Everything can be used for good or for evil. That's why Duke came here, the early 21st century: this is when time-travel was first done, in a linear timeline. He has to guard its beginnings. We can't leave the earth's fate to the schemes of any mad scientist."

Jett thought of his friend; his twinkling eyes, his inventions, the candy he always bought for Logan, the crawdads he used to catch in the creek. Teddy had given up his dream to be an astronaut and inventor to be close to Jett after Maddie's death. The least he could do for him was support him when his own dream was realized.

"I hope you don't catch him," he said frankly. "He doesn't mean any harm, only good."

"If that was the case," Parker said sadly, "Duke wouldn't be looking for him."

"This Tate fellow," Jett began, changing the subject, "Is he my real son? Or the one that the universe… invented, for lack of a better term, to solve a paradox?"

She shook her head. "No way of knowing. We can't know much, really, unless Johnson tells us. Such as the whereabouts of your other son."

Now that he had returned to the ordinary world, and was no longer under the influence of Teddy's garage, Jett began to doubt. "I'm sure Teddy's found a happy place for him, if he even exists, that is. I trust Teddy. He wouldn't hurt anybody."

"Maybe the Teddy you knew this morning," she said. "But what about Teddy after over a decade?"

Jett pressed his eyes shut. It was far past time to pick

up Logan. They needed to go fishing. And then maybe get a good night's sleep, as he had an early shift come Sunday morning.

"Can I call Tate in again?" Parker asked, simple pleading in her soft green eyes. "He wanted to tell you something."

Jett nodded.

A few moments later the boy had returned. "Mr. King," he began, but Jett cut him short.

"Please, call me Jett." It felt strange to say it, as this kid was supposed to be his son, but anything else would be even stranger.

"Well, Jett," Tate began again, "Growing up, everyone thought I was slightly…" he swallowed. "Crazy. Because of a mirror."

"A mirror?"

"It's a Voice I can hear in my head," Tate explained. "Like, telepathically, I guess. But it's like a mirror; this Voice is another version of me, or something."

"What?"

"The Voice is me!" he said earnestly. "It's me, but it's not. He thinks like me, but his feelings are a lot sadder and darker. Even though I can't really see him, like an actual mirror, I can always feel what he feels."

Jett glanced at Parker. The conversation was growing a little too weird for him. Parker nudged him and looked back to Tate.

"I was… adopted, but my mom, Sophia Emmett, loves me," Tate continued in his even, calming voice that reminded Jett of his own. "So does Dr. Emmett, and everyone I've ever met. But I get these feelings of being rejected and abused. I get horribly scared at moments when I should be enjoying my-self."

"You're saying you have some sort of connection with an-other boy in your head?" Jett asked.

"Yes, and he needs help," Tate said firmly. "He's scared and miserable. But how could I help him? I could never convince anyone that I wasn't crazy. But now, with what Parker, Duke and all the others have told me, it could be my paradox twin!"

"I'm sorry, but I have to go home." Jett pulled himself to his feet and fumbled around for his jacket. "Teddy didn't hurt anybody. Maybe you just have a strong imagination."

Parker jumped to her feet. "You can't forsake your sons!"

"I can't turn against my best friend! I can't hunt him down like a criminal. Let him travel the stars. That's all he ever wanted to do. He's gone, and there's..."

He stopped mid-sentence as two people entered the room. One was Dr. Emmett, while the other was an older woman, seemingly older than the doctor. Her facial features hinted of a part-Mexican heritage, though her eyes stood out in cold contrast, gray and piercing. Her short, dark hair was streaked with gray.

"Feeling alright?" Dr. Emmett asked. Jett nodded.

"You must be Jesse King," the woman said. Her voice was low and made Jett think of wood and trees. "I am Dr. Cariss Swusterlinn. I work with Duke."

"Pleased to meet you," Jett said, shaking her hand.

"Cariss knows your story," Parker put in, "And she was planning on helping you and Duke with the case. This is Dr. Emmett's house, and it's very close to the office. That's where you were, right, Cariss? Robbie is running calculations, and then we'll be gathering the team together to find Johnson and the other paradox twin. But Cariss, Jett thinks he can back out of it all and leave!"

"About that," Jett said, all his excuses rushing to his brain. "I may not be coming. I've got to pick up my son Logan, and I've got an early shift tomorrow, and I really don't want to go."

Cariss' piercing eyes scanned him up and down. "All right then," she said at length. "I've got it from here. If we find your other son, would you like us to notify you?"

"Yes, of course," Jett stuttered.

"Go home, then," she said. "Leave."

There was no disobeying her eyes. Jett clutched his jacket, found the door, and left.

"Cariss," Parker said urgently, "don't you think we should try to convince him to come? Not only is it his duty to find his son, but it'll be hard work tracking down Johnson without someone who knows him."

"We will not force anyone to do anything," she said, walking out of the room.

"Wait patiently, Parker," Dr. Emmett said. "Cariss knows what she's doing."

6

Famine

Centuries in the future, on a planet far from earth, Johnson sat in his cabin. He sat at his desk, rubbing the scar on his wrist absentmindedly. He had listened to Ivan and had gone to Base, where the bone had been mended with top-notch equipment in only a couple of days. Before him was an electronic pad where he had been scribbling numbers and calculations.

The planet, Reka II, was in the middle of a famine. An epidemic had wiped out their livestock and what little vegetation they had, while a fire had destroyed several of their storehouses at Base. On the electronic pad was written *5,358.* That was the number of people that lived on Reka II, and it was the number of people who were going to die if he did not do something. He shivered, and the cold pulled him out of his thoughts, and he began to scribble numbers again. It was wintertime on the planet, and the weather was severe; even in summer, Reka II's average temperature was subarctic, rarely reaching sixty degrees.

Anton stumbled in, gripping his snow-laden coat. Johnson could hear the boy scraping his feet against the mat, wiping the snow and mud off his shoes. He had sent the boy to the Communications Center to ask about the *Kenswick*, a supply ship that was headed their way with food and medical equipment to relieve them of their plight. After the hike to and from Base Anton would undoubtedly be tired, and as it was late Johnson knew he would shower and head straight to bed.

"I got you a razor, it's on the bathroom counter," said Johnson.

"But sir," Anton said, "All ze men have beards. Efen ze young men. I..."

"You look like your father. I'd like to keep it that way."

Anton almost sighed, but he caught it. "I do not even know who my father was," he said carefully, knowing he was treading dangerous waters.

Johnson shrugged, letting the comment slide. "You don't need to look like a Rekan, boy. Goodnight."

Johnson couldn't see Anton, but he knew the boy was indulging in sad puppy eyes. He never dared to make that face when he thought Johnson could see him, but the man had caught it a few times, and now could tell without looking.

Like many frustrated people before him, Anton decided to drag another long-held grievance into the discussion. "Can I cut my hair, sir?"

Johnson glanced over his shoulder. Anton had a mop of curly hair that he despised, while to Johnson it was a rare reminder of his past that he kept. "No," he answered. "But you can trim the back if you want."

Though Anton never raised his voice, it certainly got higher. "It is already trimmed in ze back! Ze back is straight! I do not mind zat! It is ze curls, zese awful curls..."

"Are you getting snippy with me?" Johnson asked, turning back to his work.

"No sir. Sorry sir." Anton began to pull off his coat.

"Any message from the *Kenswick?*" he asked, scrolling down a list of figures.

Anton's coat stopped rustling. "*Kenswick*, sir?"

Johnson lifted an eyebrow and turned in his seat. "I asked you to run down to Base and ask about the *Kenswick*."

Anton paled. "I am sorry, sir, I have not done it yet."

"Finish hanging your coat," Johnson said, attempting to keep his voice level, "And then come sit by me, Myshka."

The boy obeyed. As he settled in a wooden chair, stiff as a board, Johnson straightened himself up and folded his hands on his lap.

"Do you remember me telling you to go to Base?"

"Yes sir, I wemember now."

Something snapped inside Johnson. "Remember," he said, emphasizing the pronunciation. "*Rrr*...emember. Say that again right."

"Wemember," Anton said, his eyes frightened. "Wremmmber..."

Johnson had far too much on his mind to put up with this. He slammed his fist into the table and Anton flinched. "Remember! Forget it. Why didn't you go to Base?"

"I started, sir. I went into ze shed to get my cap. I started looking at zings and I forgot about what you said."

Johnson snatched up his electronic pad and shook it in front of Anton's face. "Five thousand people, boy, the lives of five *thousand* people are in the balance, and you spend *three hours* playing with your toys. If we all must die may justice take you first! Bring it here."

"Bring what, sir?"

"Your toy," he said through clenched teeth. "You were building something in the shed again, even though I have explicitly told you not to. We are starving to death, freezing! I want to see what was so important to you!"

Anton ran from the room. Johnson counted the seconds it would take for the boy to reach the shed, go around their car, dig out his thing from under the shelf (Anton's usual hiding place) and come back. Right on time, Anton came in shivering, his ears and cheeks flushed pink.

"Here, sir," he said, plunking a mess of metal disks, wiring plates and an ancient smartphone onto the desk. Everything seemed to be connected with wires and small glass tubes and fragile, thin circuit boards. "I had barely started. It is not much anyfing."

Johnson scanned it over. His boy was no inventor. If he pounded it once with his fist, he knew that weeks of work would be lost. Like all of Anton's contraptions, it was too complicated and too fragile, and almost certainly would never work. If the boy had shown any actual promise of talent with his inventions, Johnson might have been easier on him, but as it was Anton's work was only disobedient and distracting.

"Give me your hand," he said.

Anton held it out. Johnson grasped it with his own and

with enormous strength brought it crashing down on the device. Something shattered and a metal clip flew across the room.

"You are my *assistant*, not a *toymaker*," he shouted, smashing Anton's hand across the invention with each emphasized word. "You've *ignored* my directions *one* too many *times* but you will not *again*! You will receive *ample* punishment for this!"

Johnson let go and Anton staggered back, clutching one hand with the other. For a few moments, all was silent except their breathing: the man's heavy, gasping heaves, and the boy's quick, shivering pants.

"I am sorry, Myshka," Johnson mumbled. "I promised not to hurt you again."

"Don't worry, sir," Anton whimpered. "You didn't hurt me." The way he was clutching his hand said otherwise.

Johnson glanced at the shattered fragments. Slowly he brushed it over the edge of the desk into the wastebasket. "What... what was that invention... what was it supposed to be?"

Anton cowered. "It was not near finished, sir. It wouldn't have worked, anyway."

Nobody ever gave him a straight answer. Johnson wanted to hit something, so he chose his desk again. "What *was* it, child? Tell me now and skip the prologue!"

"I wanted to experiment wif ze space displacer formula, sir," Anton said. He was whimpering now. "It could help wif Weka's problem. But zen I got distracted coming up wif a time displacer formula instead. You are always talking about ze twenty-first century, I zought you wanted to see it."

Johnson fingered his watch. No one on Reka truly knew what it was capable of.

"No more inventions, Anton, and we'll skip your punishment," he said.

"No more inventions," Anton agreed fervently.

"I'm perfectly happy in this century," continued Johnson. "But only if we can get in contact with the *Kenswick* soon." He sighed, and pressed his fingers against his forehead. "Can I trust you to go straight to your bed?"

"Yes, sir."

"Good," Johnson said. "I see Ivan out the window; perhaps he has news of the *Kenswick*. Or maybe they've been able to subdue the force field by now."

"And if zey haven't, sir, what zen? Wemember, when we set up zat field..."

Johnson banged his fist against the desk again. "They will get through, *remember* that!"

Anton nodded before dashing into the other room.

Johnson rose and opened the door, just as Ivan approached it. The Rekan bowed and touched his forehead before stepping inside. A snug cap covered most of his head, and a scarf was wrapped around his beard, covered with little frozen droplets from his breathing. The only visible parts of his face were his red eyes, red nose, and from somewhere in his scarf his pipe protruded.

"Any news on the *Kenswick*?" Johnson asked, shutting the door.

Ivan nodded as much as he could, as his neck was stiff with cold. "It is very close, Sur Liedr," he answered. "But no matter how close it is it cannot help us if we cannot shut down ze force field."

"Didn't one of the men say they had a scientific theory for subduing force fields?"

Ivan rolled his eyes. "A theory. It has not worked."

Johnson pressed his hands against his face and paced the cabin. "I hate being locked down," he said. "We're trapped in a cage with no way of getting out. Our ships can't get out, nobody else can get in..." he touched his watch and trailed off.

Ivan grunted. "And your time-travel does not work."

"What are you talking about?" Johnson blustered.

"Don't even try to pretend. I know all about ze zings you are capable of."

Johnson glared, but he dropped his watch to his side. "Why am I not surprised?" he grumbled.

A grunt was Ivan's only response. Johnson wandered to the window, where down the mountain, across the frozen lake, was the Base. Its buildings and roads looked like toys from there. The sun was setting in that direction, just out of the window's sight, but the sky above Base was lit with brilliant colors, which drenched the snowy world below in purple and blood red. Johnson knew that in that snowy world, scientists were retiring to bed, exhausted from their studies. Soldiers and crewmen from different ships were sleeping in their bunks. And farther out, away from the Base, were the little towns with miners and civilians and their families. Madsville, Kingstown, Domzh, and behind him, in the other room, Anton was sleeping. Johnson groaned.

"I hate this accountability," he said. "And for the first time in my life I can't find a single shortcut out."

"Have you ever heard of 'facing your problems', Sur Liedr?" asked Ivan, placidly puffing.

"Don't burden me with your trite comments," Johnson snapped.

Ivan was unabashed. "We are very different, Sur Liedr. In my life before Reka, I was very good at facing my problems. I have ploughed zrough every obstacle zat has ever been in my way. For power, for glory, for me." He joined Johnson at the window. "You and I are ze leaders of zis colony. We can win zis fight, but you must change your perspective."

"What do you mean?"

"Forget about zem," he said, turning Johnson away from the window. "You cannot save everyone, so save yourself. Send more people to ze Red Planet to try shutting off ze force field."

"But they'll die," Johnson said.

Ivan shrugged. "Somebody is going to die either way. I do not want it to be me."

"You're right," Johnson said, sinking into his chair. "We have no other choice. I know the passages best, but I can't risk killing myself and robbing these people of their Liedr." He picked up his electronic pad. "I will send more men tomorrow. I want you to radio the *Kenswick* and ask if they have any way to subdue force fields."

"And when all zis is over," Ivan began, opening the door, but Johnson interrupted.

"I know, I know. I've got to remember that I made the force field with your money."

Ivan shut the door behind himself. Johnson began calculating people and food supplies, and he stayed there at his desk late into the night.

7

Impossible Things

There was a knock at office door *16*. Dr. Emmett opened it, and eyed the young man in the hallway. "What can we do for you, Jesse?" he asked.

Jett pushed his hands into his jacket pockets. "Please, call me Jett. I... is Tate here?"

Dr. Emmett shook his head. "No, he went with Duke. They went to find the paradox twin, along with Parker and Cariss."

This surprised Jett. He had never even picked up Logan, but had gone straight from the doctor's house to the creek and from the creek to the office where he was now. But they had left already. "Oh," he said, shifting his weight from one foot to the other. "May I... come in?"

Dr. Emmett shrugged. "Sure."

Jett stepped in and took a seat on the nearest chair. It was a comfortable swivel chair, though it was a little high for him. He could see Robbie's legs jutting out from underneath one of the desks, but there was no one else in the room.

There was an awkward silence, but finally Jett spoke up.

"Dr. Emmett, I wanted to speak with Tate. I wanted to tell him that I want to understand and accept him. I saw what happened to Teddy in a span of seconds, and I know time-travel is real. So I'd like to get to know Tate better and be friends."

Dr. Emmett nodded. "You do understand, of course, that he is Logan's *younger* brother?"

"Yes." Jett swallowed. "Teddy must've time-travelled backwards and somehow gotten your sister to adopt him as a baby. To line up with Tate as his father, I should be in my mid-forties. I'm twenty-eight. But I still want to be friends."

"Hmm. And what about the paradox twin?" Dr. Emmett questioned.

Jett ran his fingers through his hair. "I can't bring myself to believe he exists. The universe can't create people out of thin air. And all of Tate's nonsense about speaking to each other telepathically! He says his twin is having a miserable life, but if such a boy existed, Teddy would have looked after him. He placed Tate in a safe home, not far from me, only a few years off. He would do the same for any of my children."

Robbie tried to sit up, accidentally hitting his head against the desk. "I can't set this thing up," he grumbled. "There's a lot more to swimming through time and space than just a screwdriver and a hammer." He tossed his tools aside. "I'm not sure what Duke was thinking."

"Is Duke in a different time?" Jett asked.

"He followed Johnson's tracks to a couple hundred years into the future," Emmett explained.

Robbie scratched his head. "About that, I hope I did my

calculations right. I was using Duke's watch, and I'm not too familiar with that type of equipment. I did something, to be sure, and came up with an exact date, but I could be a week or two off. Maybe give a month; I could have been a month or two off, or a few." He paused for a moment, and then began speaking confidently again. "I know I got the sector right, though. He doesn't have too many planets he needs to comb through."

"They have it narrowed down to two stars and their orbiting planets: Reka or Epsilon," Dr. Emmett said.

"It's Reka," Jett said quietly. "For certain. Teddy named that. Reka's his middle name."

"We'd be able to tell Duke that if his useless time-displacer would work," Robbie grumbled. "Install his program, he said. If it didn't work then uninstall it and reinstall it. What use is that? And this computer is a constipated sloth if I've ever met one."

"Duke's gadgets are some of the highest technology in the present, future, or anywhere," Dr. Emmett reminded him. "The man's a genius."

"Genius! No, just lucky. Your friend Johnson must've been a genius, to invent the first time-machine," Robbie said, glancing towards Jett.

"Yes, he was. He was too clumsy and silly for anyone to ever notice, but I knew it. He was too smart for his own good." Jett sighed.

Robbie hoisted himself onto an office chair. "I wish Duke had helped me fix my ship before he left. Then we could've all gone together, in style."

"Where is your ship?" Jett asked. "How do you hide a spaceship in Nebraska?"

Robbie grinned. "It's pretty easy, actually. It's right here, in this building."

"You can't hide a spaceship in here."

"They did," Dr. Emmett said. "The original plans for this building were to have a couple offices in the basement, as well as a large meeting room, all underground. I remember when it was being built. The basement was never close to finished, though. It's nothing but a concrete hole."

Jett sucked in his breath. "You've got a spaceship under here?"

"Sure thing," answered Robbie. "Duke took the pod, which is pretty much like a lifeboat that belongs inside of my ship. We've still got the mother ship here."

"Why can't you use it?"

"Time-travel messed her up," said Robbie grimly. "It wasn't done efficiently. I've been repairing her, though. I have plenty of fuel for her, I only need to jumpstart her and make a few tweaks. I don't know where I could get a good enough power surge. Hooking her up to this building's power is the best idea I've had, but I don't think it'd be enough."

Jett leaned back in his chair and closed his eyes. He hadn't come to talk about spaceships and time-travel and impossible things. This was supposed to be a step in the direction of normal. "Doctor, tell me about Tate. What sort of boy is he?"

"Very brainy," Emmett said, with a bit of a laugh. "I can never keep up with him. Sometimes I'll be using my computer and I'll run into a little glitch, and I'll ask him to fix it. He'll come along and it seems he reprograms the whole thing!"

A smile broke across Jett's face. "He sounds a lot like Maddie."

"Now that I think of it, yes," Dr. Emmett said. "I guess he gets his personality from his mother. She would have loved him. He's a good artist, too. As a kid he always preferred paper to toys."

"Logan's like that too. He'd rather draw pictures of me in space than play with all the new cars I got him for his birthday."

"They're definitely brothers," Dr. Emmett agreed. "Tate has always wanted to be a doctor. Helping people by healing them has always been his biggest passion. He set a bone for me once."

"Really?"

Dr. Emmett smiled at the memory. "My sister and I took him on a trip to Wyoming to see some friends. A handful of us decided to take a hike into the middle of nowhere. Tate was fourteen, I think. I took a slip and dislocated a bone in my wrist. I wanted to see what he could do, so I gave him a few instructions, and he set it for me right there and wrapped it up in a splint."

A look of pain crossed Jett's face. "I... I wish I could've watched him grow up. I missed so many years. He's my son, and he's nearly an adult."

Dr. Emmett nodded. "I'm still having trouble believing he's yours and Maddie's. I know all the facts, so I know it's true, but it's a lot to take in. It's a lot of change, I guess."

"Like the paradox twin," Jett said, suddenly fretful. "If I

believe he's real, I have to go find him and everything will change!"

"Listen, Jesse," Dr. Emmett said kindly, laying a hand on his shoulder, "If I could spare you all this pain I would. You have already been through so much, with Maddie and now Teddy Johnson. We're asking you to take responsibility for two boys you never knew existed, and I know it's a lot. In a way I'm glad Tate was one of them, since I know him. But this other one is a wild card."

Jett felt hot tears against his hands. He felt horribly weak. He tried to stop the tears, but the gentle hand on his shoulder seemed to encourage him to cry. "I'm afraid you've got to face these things," the doctor continued. "You might not get much out of it for yourself, but maybe you'll do a world of good for this other twin. Compassion and kindness take a lot of work, but it's always worth it to somebody. You've got to at least look for your son. Don't you wish you could've watched him grow up?"

"Maybe," Jett said. "Maybe I do. Robbie, I need you to get me to Reka as fast as possible."

Robbie had been intensely interested in his hammer, but at the sound of his name he looked up, astonished. "Are you out of your mind? Wha'dya want Reka for?"

"I can find Teddy," Jett said, eager in his new resolve. "I know I can. We can show Duke the right planet."

Robbie lifted his hands helplessly. "I have the date and sector coordinates he used to follow Johnson, but nothing else. No ship, no time-travelling mechanism."

"Fix the spaceship," Jett urged. "Didn't you say you could jumpstart it with the power from this building?"

"Nah," Robbie answered. "The power is too weak. If I drained the entire city of power for a little while, then…" he stopped and his eyes lit up. "Doctor, you know this town. How are power lines set up in the twenty-first century? Are they connected?"

"I don't know much about it," Dr. Emmett confessed.

"If the power goes out, does your neighbor's go with it?" Robbie pushed.

"Yes," Jett said.

"I'm going to go have a look!" Robbie exclaimed, grabbing his coat and dashing out the door.

"I have the feeling that my uncle at the IT office will not appreciate this," Jett said. He turned to the doctor. "Do we have a time-travelling machine? We'll use the ship to fly there, but we've got to get into the future."

"His ship can do it," Dr. Emmett answered. "There are two ways to time-travel: mechanically, and organically. One is cheating, the other is a mystery."

"By organically," said Jett, "I hope you don't mean waiting hundreds of years in linear time."

"No, no. Did Duke ever tell you about his powers?"

Jett shook his head. "Not in full. Does it have something to do with his eyes?"

Emmett thought for a moment. "I think so," he said. "I'm not sure of who or what he is, but I know what he can do. Time-travel comes as easily as thinking to him. Sometimes I wonder if he's even from our universe."

Jett began envisioning time-travelling aliens, which in his head looked a lot like clocks with legs. "So he can time-travel just by thinking?"

"It's even more complicated than that. He can't always control his power, and he accidentally time-travels to random places. If that happens, you'll see him glow like fire, and before you know what's happening he's gone. He always reappears seconds later. He speaks of time as if it were a river he's fallen into, and it constantly throws him around."

"So time controls him, not the other way around."

Dr. Emmett nodded. "In a way. I think there's something wrong between him and time. His timeline isn't steady. So like I said, if you ever see him disappear, don't worry. He'll be back in a few moments. He slips in and out of the past and the future a lot."

"But can he control time-travel and make it useful? Is his way more effective than, say, Teddy's way of doing it?"

"Compared to anything normal humans could do he has unheard of power. Rough, raw, but beautiful power. He travels time as he pleases and he can walk through minds and memories."

Jett shuddered. Dr. Emmett touched his shoulder.

"And he made a key for Robbie's spaceship. It looks like a key, underneath a strong, clear case on the control board, but don't ever open it and touch it. Duke says it might erase you from time. But it's the organic way of travelling I mentioned: we can fly through time on Duke's stored energy. But only if we can get the ship off the ground."

The door burst open. Robbie's eyes were shining. "I think we got a chance," he said.

8

The Starlight

Jett followed the two men out into the hallway and down the stairwell. On the bottom floor, they went down a drab passage and came to an insignificant looking door, tucked away in a corner. It required a code to open. Robbie punched in *7777* and they were in.

It opened up to a dark, narrow staircase. When Dr. Emmett shut the door behind them, it locked and shut out all light. There were odd dripping noises from above, the walls were moist, and the wooden steps felt rotten. Jett covered his nose to avoid the smell of mildew as they descended.

At last the stairs ended, and before them was a wide, open space. It was too dark to tell how big the basement was, but Jett could sense plenty of room, and could see flashes of it from a pocket-light Dr. Emmett produced. There was a strong smell of something like diesel oil. Jett heard a *click* and the overhead lights turned on.

Robbie's spaceship was about as long as three vans parked end to end. The front half was a rounded semi-circle, painted a light gold color with black squares across the front. The back end was more boxy in shape, but it was still sleek with a streamlined flare. *Starlight 3000* was written across it in bold letters. It was not anything like what Jett had imagined, but more simple and oddly shaped.

"Does it take off like a rocket?" he asked, eyeing the craft, "or a plane, or a helicopter? And how can that thing withstand zero gravity and radiation and..."

"Welcome to the future." Robbie cut him off with a wink. "I've got her connected to this city's electricity. It might be the boost she needs."

Jett noticed a thick wire running down the stairs and disappearing behind the spaceship. He could have tripped on it and broken his neck on the stairs. Robbie did not seem too concerned about safety hazards.

"You can't take off here," Dr. Emmett pointed out. "You'd blast this building to smithereens. I know Duke was able to displace the pod, but all we've got is the time-key, which can't move the location of this thing. We'll never get it to a good place for takeoff."

"Never say never," Robbie answered. He touched the side and a hidden door slid open. Jett stepped in, and found himself in the control room. At the back end, there was a line of plush chairs, and he quickly sank into one, looking around. Large viewing screens lined the rounded front of the control room, and right now they showed a dank wall, exactly as windows would have. Four chairs, connected firmly to the floor, were up by the control panels. The panels twinkled with buttons, levers and mini-screens. The room lost its curve near the back with the line of seats where Jett was. The line was only broken by a door that led to the back room of the craft.

Robbie came in a few moments later. "Get ready for a ride," he said, flipping a lever and adjusting a few controls.

"This is not how I imagined a futuristic spaceship," Jett confessed, glancing around for a seatbelt. He couldn't find one. "It's not very big. No second deck, or anything."

"She's a racer, not a freight-tub," Robbie huffed. "It's meant for one or two pilots to fly at an incredibly fast speed. I could warp this thing into oblivion." He stroked the pilot seat.

"How come there are four seats there at the controls?"

Robbie shrugged. "She flies best with two pilots. For extra hard races, there's only one. The other seats are usually reserved for a judge or two, who make sure everyone is playing fair and keep track of speed and technique. And sometimes the racing contestant will take his sweetheart with him, he's got to have a place to put her, hasn't he?"

"And these seats back here?"

"Audience. Critics. Media. Peanut gallery."

There was a sharp buzz. "The doctor must be touching the door," Robbie explained. "That buzz lets me know someone is trying to get in. I need to find a way to unlock it without my fingerprint." He gave the wall a pat as he walked past and then busied himself at some of the controls.

The door opened at his touch, and Dr. Emmett stepped in. "I set the devices where you wanted them, Robbie. What are you doing?"

"It's a special feature on the *Starlight*," Robbie explained, touching buttons. None of them required pressing, so his fingers flew across the panel as if he were playing a very sensitive piano. "It has a field-displacer. It's normally shut off and locked, though. I'm trying to override the system."

"What does it do?" asked Jett.

Robbie rolled his eyes. "Displaces the field, of course. Namely, itself. I'm trying to beam us… there."

He looked up at the screens along the wall. The view of the basement had vanished. Instead there was an overhead picture of a large, empty plain.

"No one will see us there," Robbie said. "I can take off, and when I get too close to whatever satellites you've got out there I can beam us out of this solar system. I won't try much farther than that, though. I don't want to strain you, *Star*."

The viewing screens returned to the wall. Robbie sat down in the pilot's seat and began to work. The ship began to hum. Jett suddenly began to imagine a co-pilot in the next seat, dressed in a fancy jacket, engaging the displacer with a grin of confidence towards his comrade. He could see judges, taking notes and whispering while they waited for the real show to begin. The ship's hum grew louder, and the picture grew clearer in Jett's mind. The back wall was full of reporters, snapping photos, and rich people who thrilled to watch races. A sweetheart stood behind the pilot, encouraging him in his ear. The air was thick with expectation, and the deep yearning of a pilot to race in space grew with every thrum of the engine. And then suddenly the humming of the ship stopped. Jett blinked, and the images were gone. Robbie looked strange by himself, with three empty seats beside him.

"Come on, *Star*, I've got ya," Robbie said, frowning at the controls.

Jett leaned back in his chair. The image had been very real and vivid, as if it were a memory of what this ship had known before that still lingered behind, a living ghost of the past. For the first time, he was truly curious about where Robbie and the *Starlight* had come from. "Where did you get this ship?" he asked at length. The *Starlight* was quiet, and Robbie was trying to wake it up from the panels.

"I was living in a Melville slum," Robbie answered, only giving some of his attention. The ship began to hum again under his coaxing. "To earn my living I was working at a college. I kept the place clean and all that nonsense." His voice trailed off as he adjusted his coordinates.

"Could you not afford to attend college? Or have a decent home?" Jett asked. He didn't mean to be so blunt, but he asked before he could think about it much.

"I was trying to explain the *Starlight*, not me," Robbie grumbled. "But the truth is, they wouldn't have let me into college if I had tried. I'm from the far-off future, even farther than where we're going today, and in my day I'm an outcast. I was born in the streets and I have no way of proving I'm clean-blooded. I could have Moonseye. I probably do."

"What's that?"

"A mutation of sorts," Robbie said. "Sicknesses and disease aren't any prettier in my day than in yours, and we also have a host of horrid things explorers brought back from space." The spaceship began to rumble. Robbie frowned, and increased the input of electricity. "Everybody just lost power."

"How did you learn to pilot a spaceship?"

"I listened in on the piloting classes at the college where I worked. That's the only reason I took the job at all. My type isn't supposed to learn, but I learned anyway. But one day I snuck into a hangar where they were storing a few ships for the big race. I just wanted a peek. They had a fancy beast all the way from New France, but I wasn't interested in her. I knew this one, *Starlight 3000*, would win. I befriended an engineer there and managed to borrow his list of passwords and codes."

The ship began to creak and groan. "There's something wrong with the output of the power cells," he said, sounding stressed. "Come on *Starlight*. You can do it. You can make it."

"You stole the codes because you wanted to have a peek inside," Jett surmised.

"Yeah. And that's when I ran into this fellow named Johnson."

Jett's heart skipped a beat.

"I'm pretty sure he was trying to steal it, like I told you before," Robbie said, sliding off his chair onto his knees to reach under the panels. He began feeling around and rearranging wires. "Johnson pretended to be an engineer doing some maintenance for the race. So did I. We both knew the other didn't belong there."

The ship's groaning stopped. Instead, it began to screech. It sounded like an old train letting off steam.

Robbie gritted his teeth. "Come on."

"Teddy must've tried to send it back to the 21st century, or whatever century he's in now," Jett guessed.

Robbie nodded, getting back into his seat. "Yup. Of course he said it was part of the maintenance. I helped him out and could tell he was doing something fishy. It backfired on him, though. It worked before it was supposed to. While he was beside it fiddling with his wires he flung it back in time, with me in it. Duke found me and placed the ship here."

The ship gave a violent jerk. Jett was thrown onto the floor, his head bashing against the wall. All of the lights flickered off for a moment, but as the spaceship settled, they turned back on. All was eerily silent; no screeching, no groaning, only a gentle humming noise. Jett rose to his feet, his heart beating quickly, and his eyes were drawn to the viewing screens.

They were on an endless plain.

"Hurrah Nebraska!" Robbie clamped down a lever and with a gentle whoosh, the spaceship rose. It reminded Jett of when he had once ridden in the police helicopter, only smoother. They glided upwards, Robbie retracted the landing gear, and then they rushed towards the clouds. In the corner of his consciousness, right where no amount of looking could see, Jett could hear the cheers of the audience, the whoops of the pilot, the chatter of the news-people. The judges were scoring the takeoff and the sweetheart was shrieking with pride. Jett blinked and they were gone.

"Hold on, gentlemen," Robbie said, alone in his seat.

There was another jolt, and another temporary loss of light. Jett had grasped the sides of his chair, but he was still jerked out and slammed into the floor. With an aching head, he pulled himself up.

"*Starlight*, you're a wonder," Robbie praised.

Jett turned to the screen. The plains were gone, replaced by a black sea of glittering lights. They were flying into the stars.

"This ship almost seems to have a consciousness of its own," Dr. Emmett said thoughtfully. He was sitting beside Jett, who had nearly forgotten he was there. "It has a strange effect on a person."

"That she does," Robbie said absentmindedly. "An effect I rather like." He cleared his throat and glanced at a mini-screen. "I've set the key with Duke's coordinates. We're in the future, now. Landscape looks about the same." He squinted at the vast array of stars. "Now all we've got to do is warp to Reka."

"And what is warp?" asked Jett.

"It's a bubble in space, I guess, that lets us go faster than the speed of light. I know how to use it, but if you want the fancy equations you'll have to find someone with real schooling."

Dr. Emmett leaned forwards. "Now that we're in the same time, shouldn't our communicators work with Duke's?"

Robbie grabbed a small device, like a shiny walkie-talkie, and tossed it back. Dr. Emmett caught it. "There's the Hiero, doc. But we're probably out of range, they're several sectors away. Try in half an hour."

"I guess it'll be a little while then," Jett said. "Dr. Emmett, what exactly does your little group do? Duke, Parker, and all them?"

"Duke is from this century, I believe, the 23rd. He offered

his services to the Space Agency, but apparently time-travel is the same myth in their time as it is in ours. But when Duke proved to them that it was possible, the Agency decided to send him on missions to monitor the use of time-technology."

"There must be others who have done it besides Teddy," Jett said.

"Yes, but what makes it worse is that it has always been a secret deed. Duke has not yet found a time period that realizes time-travel has been done. It's the secret few who can do it, but sometimes they try to manipulate it for themselves and cause problems."

"But how does he find them?"

Dr. Emmett shrugged. "I honestly don't know. I believe he has his own ways."

Jett glanced towards the viewing screens, where there was nothing but stars. He wondered if Robbie knew how to find his way around the galaxy. "Robbie told me his story," Jett said softly. "I suppose that after Duke found him, he asked him to be an assistant of sorts?"

Dr. Emmett snorted. "Robbie *begged*. He didn't want to go back to his own time, so Duke lets him hang around. I believe our boy-pilot is living a dream he never knew was possible."

Jett smiled in spite of himself. "And what about the rest of you? Why was Parker at the office?"

Dr. Emmett smiled. "We're all random people who have met at random times. Parker has an interesting story that has not been explained yet. She came searching for Duke, saying that she'd been told by a time-traveller to find him. Duke isn't sure of what happened, but he says we'll understand it eventually. Parker's glad she found someone to believe her. She's got a job in Angel, but she spends her free time pestering Duke with questions and helping him write a report to bring back to the Agency."

"And what about you and Cariss?"

"I've known Cariss for years professionally, ever since she moved here and started practice. She introduced me to Duke when he was looking for a bed, food, and a friend. I don't know how Cariss met him. I guess you can say I'm part of the team because I'm the only one who has ever believed them."

"I believe them, now," Jett said. He sighed and changed the subject. "What are we going to do when we find Teddy?"

"This is the 23rd century," Emmett said. "Duke's century, and the century of the Space Agency. Johnson has committed several crimes in this time-period. Duke intends to hold him accountable for that and for the paradox he created with your sons."

"Teddy isn't a criminal," Jett said. "Perhaps he got a little carried away with his time-travel, but he isn't a criminal."

9

Light and Silence

Ahead of the *Starlight*, out of reach by radar and radio, was the shuttle pod. Inside, it was a cramped, round room, as the pod was usually used either for storage or as a lifeboat of sorts if the mother ship failed. Duke and Cariss sat at the controls. They were a stark contrast as a pair. Duke was simmering, the same creature he had been when he had approached Teddy Johnson about his time-travel. His eyes were flaming, his forehead was creased, and he was gripping a lever with an intensity that turned his knuckles white.

Cariss sat as if she were carved from stone, her gray-streaked hair and piercing eyes adding to the effect. Her face was empty, a perfect mask to hide whatever thoughts were on her mind. Behind the pair, Parker and Tate sat squeezed together on the single seat, their hearts thumping. Neither had ever imagined travelling through the stars before, but here they were.

"We're getting close to both Epsilon and Reka," Cariss said, checking a navigation chart on a mini-screen.

Duke gazed at the viewing screen. The endlessness of

space gazed back at him. He had conflicting ideas on which planet Johnson had run to. When he had been given the mission, the details had been vague, but Duke had a suspicion that his higher-ups had known a lot more than they let on. "Let me think," he said. He released the controls and grabbed his hair instead, bowing his head, losing himself in thought.

Wordlessly, Cariss stopped the pod's progress. "Can you believe it?" Parker whispered to Tate. "We're in a little ship, floating around in space. I never imagined there would be so much color and light."

"It's an experience, that's for sure," Tate said.

They went silent. On the viewing screen, the stars blazed, flaming and alive, sending out rays and images of indescribable colors that wove around them and the shuttle and the distant galaxies. The colors were ones we have all seen in dreams, but ones that never seem to have a match in the waking world. The stars and their rays stood there, suspended in space, never moving and never speaking. It was a world that had never heard a human voice. Several ships, made by man, had passed through the ranks of these ancient stars, but they were merely contained bubbles, not daring to intrude upon the ageless silence. No noise had ever been made before the shining, glorious faces of the stars, over the thousands of years they had been there. It was a solemn light that knew only innocence and silence.

At length, Cariss spoke. "Duke, perhaps you could use your watch to look for time-displacement. That would lead us to Johnson, wherever he may be."

Parker had learned by now that Duke's watch merely reflected Duke's own senses and powers. Duke could sense time-travel, like a bloodhound could smell a scent, and his watch was a tool that could echo what he felt. Tate did not know as much about it yet, but he could tell that whatever Duke's powers were, at the present moment he had little control over them.

"I tried," Duke said, his voice weary. "But the readings are everywhere. I think they're pointing to Epsilon, but that can't be right, can it? The Agency told me Johnson was the president of Reka. I can't feel time right now, not after the jump I did to get us here. I've gone numb except for my head. My head... I'm in pain."

"Keep control over yourself," she said sternly. "You can fight pain. You should never feel it. I don't want you accidentally flinging yourself into the Middle Ages again. Sit up and look at the screens."

"Last I checked, I was the one giving orders," Duke snapped. The fire in his eyes was feverishly bright. His head ached, and he was catching glimpses of other people's thoughts and different places throughout Time.

"Duke," Parker said sweetly, "I think you should calm down. What you said to Cariss wasn't kind at all. We aren't going to get anywhere if..."

Duke flared up. "Quiet!" he shouted. "We aren't getting anywhere if you keep talking. Don't tell me what to do!"

"Duke," Cariss said, raising her voice commandingly. "Stop. You're only harming yourself. Not another word, except an apology to Parker."

Her voice absorbed his fire instantly. His eyes dropped to subdued coals, and he sat in his seat, clutching his hair and shivering. The thoughts and places in his mind passed, and the numbness faded away.

"Forgive me, Parker," he said.

"That's all right," Parker answered, still startled by his rapid changes.

"Tate, can you hear anything from the paradox twin?" asked Cariss, changing the subject smoothly.

Tate shrugged. "It's like a dark mirror, Cariss. Sometimes I can see his mind, sometimes I can't, and sometimes I think I mistake my own thoughts for his, though every now and then it's the other way around. There isn't much right now."

"The thing is, Tate, that your thoughts and his thoughts line up at the same age," said Duke. "Wherever this twin is in time or space, if he is ten years, three months and twenty seconds, that's the one you were connected to when you were that exact age. But because of time-travel, if your twin is out here, there's no knowing whether we'll first meet him as a five-year-old or a grown man."

Cariss frowned at one of her screens. "Duke, we're picking up a signal from one of the planet systems."

"Which one? What does it say?" Duke asked, immediately alert and focused on the trail.

"One of the Reka planets, Reka II, specifically, is sending a code one alert. It's being broadcasted repeatedly throughout this sector, so any ship in this area will pick it up. According to the message date, they've been sending this for months now."

"What sort of message?" Parker asked.

"It's a cry for help," Cariss answered. "The planet is in an emergency state and has been for a while, judging from this message."

"Cariss, look at this," Duke exclaimed. "Another ship is in near proximity to us, getting closer every second."

There was a Hiero radio between them, and suddenly it began to crackle and speak. "Captain Robbie Finley to shuttle pod," a voice sang out. "Come in, shuttle pod."

Duke grabbed the radio. "How on earth did you manage to get out here?"

"The city's power, a field displacer, and then your key," Robbie answered. "I can explain it more in a minute. For now, you should put the pod back in here. I'm opening the shaft, lock onto my position and it should fly right in."

Cariss had been running her hands over the controls. "Done," she said. "We're headed that way."

"This pod belongs in Robbie's ship, doesn't it?" Parker asked.

"Yes," Duke answered. "It fits nicely into the back, and once we're in we can shut it off and leave these controls completely. We'll be in the *Starlight* with the others."

Moments later, the pod was safely in the back of the ship. "Hang on a minute," Robbie instructed over the radio. "I've got to adjust the pressure and pump oxygen into the cracks. The door will unlock in a second and you'll be in."

The viewing screens and glittering buttons began to power off, and soon they were left in complete darkness. There was a whooshing noise, barely audible, and then the door swung open by itself. Duke, Cariss, Parker and Tate stepped into the *Starlight's* control room, blinking at the sudden light.

"Welcome aboard," Robbie greeted, glancing over his shoulder with a grin. "I will be your pilot, and our destination is Reka, which was chosen by our honored passenger, Jett King. We even have a doctor, in case you need one."

"Let's hope you don't," Dr. Emmett said.

"If Mr. King says Reka is the place, then full speed ahead, Robbie," Duke said.

"Call me Jett, please," Jett put in.

"Of course, sorry." Duke lowered his voice. "Thanks for being here, Jett." He moved on, sitting at the controls beside Robbie, and Cariss joined them. Parker and Tate settled themselves in the back beside Dr. Emmett and Jett King.

The *Starlight* sped through the stars, coursing through the very veins of space. The stars shone, twinkling with the brilliance of every color wrapped up in a prism of white. It was a light that revealed everything, and under its effect Jett began to lose sight of all his fears. He felt nothing but warmth, geniality, and, strangely, shame; but this faded away after a while.

All the persons on board began to talk and laugh as if they had known each other for years. Parker told of the sun in Georgia, and Tate talked of syringes and his own theories on blood clotting. Dr. Emmett told them the story of a difficult patient. Robbie explained some of the controls, and demonstrated how he could use them even without pressing them, but by connecting his hand to what he called a *partem sensor*.

Duke and Cariss spoke little, but the former would still comment and smile.

At length they came upon the Reka system, and everyone hushed. The view through the screens was ominous. So far they had travelled through brilliant light, but before them was a single star, dim and colorless. It was surrounded by a ring of darkness. The star Reka and its planets Reka I and II were home to another hub of human civilization, but from their distance it seemed to be a dark hole in the fabric of space.

"The view of the stars from the planet must be amazing," Duke commented, "But from the stars looking in, this is a rather black system, blacker than most."

"It's the sort of darkness that makes one think he can do whatever he pleases without a soul ever knowing," Dr. Emmett said thoughtfully.

Parker shuddered. "After all that light, I don't like this at all."

Cariss frowned at one of her screens. "There's a force field ahead, Duke. It's impossible to enter the orbit of either of the planets unless it's shut down. My radar is also picking up another vessel, in the same proximity to the force field as us. It's not moving."

"What vessel? Run it through my computer," Duke said.

"Just did. It's the *SS Kenswick*. Apparently it's a supply ship, a freighter of sorts."

"It must be trapped outside the force field as well," Duke said thoughtfully.

"What's a force field?" Jett asked, walking up to the four front seats.

"A field of energy," explained Cariss. "For this planet, it's like a locked door. We can't enter this star's system unless the people on Reka shut it down. According to your computer, Duke, only one of the planets is inhabited: Reka II. It's still sending out a distress signal, but it also has that force field up, so no one can get in."

"But we have to get in to find Johnson and the paradox twin," Dr. Emmett said.

Parker looked worried. "If we radio to ask them to shut down the force field, Johnson would know we were coming."

Robbie shook his head. "Force field, no problem. My space-displacer can zap us right past it. It's futuristic technology that I don't suppose they have in this century."

"It's 2254, so you're right. Our furthest technology is teleporting single people at a time," Duke said. "But your space-displacer is just what we need. We don't want to risk calling in and asking Reka II to lower their force field so we'll jump right past it. But what is the *Kenswick* doing there? Why isn't the planet letting them in?"

Robbie shrugged. "Dunno, maybe we'll find out. Take a seat, everyone, we're going space hopping. It might be a little bumpy."

10

Communications Center

Down on Reka II, Johnson had left his cabin and was in the Communications Center at Base. He was in the computer room, which was a long, rectangular shape with a low ceiling. One wall was a steady line of desks covered with computers and radios. Besides Johnson, a crowd of men filled the room, along with Ivan and Anton. There were chairs and tables scattered about, but everyone was huddled by a desk. The lights were dim, nearly hiding their figures as they crowded around a computer screen.

"It's Kingstown," one of the men said grimly. He had a dark beard and pinched cheeks. "Ze message is nearly in."

They waited impatiently for it to process. They had limited technology on Reka II, and what they had was slow and outdated. They had never had a real radio connection with Earth or any other system, and the connection between the different towns on their own planet was sketchy.

Suddenly the message appeared in full. "They're asking

about food again," Johnson said after scanning it. "Ivan, send them a response in the negative."

"Yes, Sur Liedr," Ivan answered.

"Are you sure zis is ze right zing to do?" one of the men asked anxiously. His thin frame was wrapped in a bulky coat. "It is lying."

"What ozer option do we have?" said another. "We need ze food so we can work on getting ze *Kenswick* in."

"But zey are begging for food, and we were never just in ze first place. It will be a bit of a scandal," the other man said.

Ivan shook his head. "If I may interrupt, according to our calculations, if ze food consumption here at Base and ze surrounding village continues at ze same rate, we have food for anozer zree days. Ze *Kenswick* has asked for a week to work on reducing ze energy of our force field. We could manage to keep ourselves and ze village fed, possibly. Only Kingstown and Madsville have submitted problems as to serious shortage."

By *serious shortage*, the others knew he meant that Kingstown and Madsville were the towns with the most deaths so far. A shiver ran through the group, but in the dark no one could clearly see the face of another. "Send them the message, Ivan," Johnson ordered, pushing his chair away and rising to his feet. "Tell them we're out of food. Send them our condolences as to their situation and our brightest hopes. And then, gentlemen, let's step into the briefing room. We must come up with a solution to bring down that force field. Perhaps another visit to Reka I, the Red Planet, is in order."

Another man raised his hand. "Sur Liedr, should I stay behind and monitor ze *Kenswick's* frequency?"

Johnson shook his head. "They won't call for a while. There's no way they could've made any progress." He paused as a suspicion entered his mind. "I hope you are not trying to skip out on our meeting. The Red Planet is something to fear, but I should hope my men aren't cowards."

"We can't leave ze lines unattended." The man shifted from one foot to another.

"Anton?" Johnson turned around.

The boy was leaning against the doorway. "Yes sir?"

"Monitor the frequency," Johnson said. "We'll be in the next room."

Anton nodded. "Yes sir."

The group of men, their faces still shadowed by the semi-darkness, filed out of the room. After a few minutes, Ivan rose and followed them. Anton groped for the switch and raised the brightness, though he knew they were trying to conserve electricity, and then sat down at the desk and folded his hands in his lap. He could hear the hum of the men's voices in the other room, but could not distinguish what they were saying.

After a while, he ran a frequency search out of boredom. The *Kenswick* showed up clearly, not trying to send a message, but keeping the frequency running to stay in contact with the colony below. All of a sudden, a strange signal showed up on his scan. His eyes widened. Quickly he opened up the new channel.

"Robert Juno Finley, captain of the *Starlight 3000*, requesting permission to land," a clear voice sliced through the room.

Anton pressed a button. "Zis is Anton Venedict," he said, his voice tinged with hope. "I did not notice you on our wadar until now, sir. How did you get past ze force field?"

"It's a trick of mine," the captain answered.

"You are a miracle, sir," Anton exclaimed. "I will check ze landing field." He flicked on a viewing screen. The landing field, which was outside of the Base's walls, was empty. He flipped on a switch that turned on the warning lights around it and then returned to the radio. "All is clear, sir. Go ahead and land. We have not had visitors in many monfs. I will call our Sur Liedr Johnson, or president in English, wight away to greet you."

"Hold on a moment," the captain said. "You might want to monitor my landing. Flying's a bit rough, with the force field above us. And I've never landed here before. If you could keep an eye on me it would be a lifesaver."

"Of course," the boy answered. "Ze warning lights are on, ze way is clear. I am watching, I have you on wadar and my screens."

"Thank you, kind sir," the captain said. "I'm coming down."

Anton watched with wide eyes as the sleek craft eased onto the landing platform, quicker and smoother than any of the ships he was accustomed to in the 23rd century. "Zat ship is a beauty, sir," he said admiringly. "Let me put you in our logs. It's procedure before you unboard. Captain Wobert Finley, you said?"

"Robert Juno Finley, yes," the captain affirmed. "Put her down as the *Starlight 3000*. Now, could you update me as to your situation? We noticed your emergency signals, and thought we'd drop in to see if we could be of any service."

"Yes sir, we are in a bad way," replied Anton. "Have you heard of ze spotted fly epidemic?"

"No, I'm not usually in this sector."

"Ah. If you are from Earf you would not know it. All of our crops and livestock have been dead for monfs. Some of our storage food was spoiled, and some of ze warehouses were caught in fires. We have eaten nearly all zat is left."

"Hmm. My crew and I would be glad to help. Permission to enter Base?"

Anton typed a code into the computer. "Permission. Ze Gate is unlocked."

"Thank you. Captain out."

Anton pushed his chair back and jumped to his feet. He whirled around right as Johnson and the rest of the committee entered. "A ship has gotten zrough," he exclaimed, nearly bouncing in his excitement. "Zey know how to get zrough ze force field!"

Johnson's heart leapt at the prospect of freedom. "Is it true?" He turned his eyes to the computer screen, and saw the *Starlight 3000* resting on the landing platform. He paused, wondering why he remembered that ship. But then watched as Duke, Jett, and the others began to unload.

His face blanched. The vortex manipulator on his wrist did not work inside the force field. He was trapped.

"You wretched child!" he shouted, clutching Anton by the

throat. He slammed the boy against the wall. "You were never given permission to admit anybody! You should've called me! How dare you take things into your own hands!"

"Johnson!" Ivan shouted, trying to get between them. "Isn't zis what we wanted, a ship to break zrough?"

"I know these people," Johnson raged. "They aren't here to help, they're here to destroy this colony and carry your Sur Liedr away. We've got to stop them, now!"

The men took his word for it. "Arm yourselves with pistols, men," Ivan ordered. "We must surprise zese newcomers and lock zem up before any trouble is caused."

"And you," Johnson said, casting furious eyes toward Anton, "I don't know who you think you are. You've endangered our entire community."

Anton's eyes widened. "But sir, I zought…"

"Out of my sight, now!" Johnson ordered. Ivan handed him a pistol, and he turned to face the men. "Follow my lead. Let's stop these intruders!"

11

Hopeless

Out in the landing field, Duke, Cariss, Dr. Emmett, Jett, Robbie, Parker and Tate stepped out of the *Starlight* and onto the snowy landscape of Reka II. On one side of them was the Base. It was a cluster of low buildings, covering maybe a mile, surrounded on all sides by a nine-foot steel fence. In the other direction there was a breathtaking view of a frozen lake, sparkling like a diamond in the snow. There were several snug houses around it, not much different from houses you would see on Earth, with smoke rising from the chimneys. Above them towered the mountains.

Paved roads broke away from the Base and the houses in several directions, and while some of them were covered with snow, others had been recently cleared and they cut like black lines across the white ground. Not a soul was in sight. It was dusk, but millions of stars cast an ethereal glow which the snow reflected, giving them enough light to see by.

The seven of them walked across the landing platforms and up to Base. A huge gate barred the way, large enough to admit a vehicle. Robbie pushed it open without difficulty, as Anton had unlocked it from the Communications Center. "It's colder and quieter in here," Robbie commented as they stepped inside. Even inside Base, where there were cars, a road, and numerous buildings, there was not a person to be seen.

"With this much progress on the planet, there should always be people bustling around," Cariss observed. "The famine must be serious."

"I wonder who the boy on the radio was, and where he is," Dr. Emmett said. "I imagine he would send somebody out to greet us, but this place seems deserted."

Duke's eyes were blazing again. He pointed to a low, long building, cream-colored with blue lettering. "Communications Center. Let's go."

They cut across the road. Behind them, the gate swung shut of its own accord and locked with a *clang*. The path to the building was covered with brown snow, trampled down and layered with boot prints. As they drew nearer to the Center, an unseen voice called out to them.

"Stop where you are," the voice barked in a harsh, foreign accent. "You are surrounded. Attempt to run and you will taste our weapons."

"They sure threw out the welcoming mat for us," said Robbie.

Dr. Emmett glanced around. "We came to help," he called. "You sent out a distress signal, didn't you?"

Two figures rose from behind a concrete bench. One had a dark beard and red eyes, and he held a sort of pistol in his hand. The other man was Teddy Johnson.

"You!" Johnson fumed, directing his words at Duke. "You think you can drag me off now, while my people are dying and I am defenseless! The nerve! The cruelty! You will never lay your hands on me!"

Duke's voice was edged with heat. "You must answer for your crimes!"

Mercy!" wailed Johnson. "Mercy! At least save Reka!"

Duke walked toward him, each step crunching in the muddy snow. His eyes were flickering. "You showed no mercy to time. We came here for you, not Reka."

"Duke, wait!" Parker exclaimed. "We can help him first, can't we?"

"One hundred and nine dead," Johnson shouted. "Starved and frozen to death, men, women, children. And you'd pluck the leader from these people, when they need him most?"

"The damage you've done to time is what I'm concerned about," Duke said in a voice of fire that wasn't quite his own.

Simultaneously, he and Johnson whipped out their pistols. Duke's had been hidden inside his coat, and it was a weapon similar to the ones on Reka. Both guns sent a stream of red laser, and nearly at the same moment both men were hit and knocked into the snow.

Duke landed on his knees. From inside out, an unnatural fire burned visibly where he had been hit. Shaking with pain, he aimed his pistol again. But before he could fire, Jett gave him a firm kick, hitting him in the back and pushing him face-first into the snow. He stomped on Duke's wrist, and the gun slipped out his hand.

"That's enough," said Jett. He looked across at Ivan, and several other men who had stepped out of their hiding places, holding weapons and eyeing their fallen leader. "Enough, all of you! We want to help. Drop the guns."

The Rekans hesitated.

"Drop them!" Jett said. He stooped and picked up Duke's pistol and flung it aside. It hit a clump of snow and disappeared noiselessly. "I hear one hundred and nine are dead, isn't that enough?"

One by one, the pistols clattered onto the pavement or dropped into the snow. Jett walked down the pathway and held his hand out to Ivan. "I'm Jesse King. We'd like to help, if we can."

Ivan's eyes shifted nervously, and he kept his hands at his sides. "I am Ivan Koswitch. I am ze vice president of Reka. Pleasure to meet you. What did ze ozer man mean, about Johnson's crimes?"

Jett hesitated. "I believe Teddy's been called to appear before a court or something."

"No!" Johnson had lain prostrate up to this point, but now he staggered onto his knees. In a flash he was on his feet and climbing up the steps leading to the door of the Center. He waved his pistol in his hand. "You will never touch me, Jesse!"

Suddenly he slipped on ice. With a cry, he tumbled down the concrete steps, crashing against a bench at the bottom.

Tate was watching Dr. Emmett care for Duke, but without hesitation he left them and knelt beside Johnson.

"He seems to have a guilty conscience," Ivan said. For now, it seemed safer to play on the newcomers' side than Johnson's. "But he does not matter right now. We are dying, and we must accept your help no matter ze conditions. How did you get zrough ze force field?"

"Field displacer," Robbie piped up. "It hasn't been invented yet, but I'd be happy to use it to help you if I can."

"Hold it," a tremulous voice interrupted. Everyone turned towards the Center.

Anton was in the doorway, clutching a pistol. His eyes were bloodshot and his face was pale, and his free hand was clutching his shoulder where he had been pushed against the wall. His curly hair was matted to his forehead with sweat.

"Son, we're going to…" Jett began, but Anton cut him off.

"You." He pointed his weapon at Tate. "Hands off ze man."

Tate rose to his feet slowly, holding up his hands. "I was only helping him."

"You are a miracle, Myshka," Johnson mumbled weakly. "Keep them here until I'm gone."

Anton nodded. "Yes sir."

Johnson stood and staggered around the building and out of sight.

Tate pressed his lips together, and then made a reckless dash after him. Anton fired a shot that went wide and chipped a concrete bench. Jett jumped up the porch steps and tackled the boy to the ground.

The pistol clattered down the steps. Ivan picked it up, turned it over in his hands, and then tossed it into the snow. Jett stood up and offered a hand to Anton. Hesitantly, the boy took it.

"You look like you could use some medical attention," Jett commented. "My friend is a doctor. He'll help you."

Anton didn't move or speak. His curls were in his eyes, which were wide with silent fright.

"How old are you?" Jett asked kindly.

"Sixteen today, sir," he stammered.

"I hope your birthday improves." Jett turned to face his friends and the Rekans. He raised his voice so they could all hear. "Let's go inside. I want to hear what's wrong and how we can fix it. Robbie, help Dr. Emmett bring Duke in."

"What about Tate?" Parker asked.

"He'll be fine," Jett assured her. "Teddy was unarmed and injured. We'll go after them later. Teddy would never hurt one of my sons." He turned back to Anton. "Let me help you in. Lean on me."

Duke, meanwhile, was sitting in the snow shivering. "Give me a hand up, Robbie."

"Are you sure you can stand?" Robbie said doubtfully.

"I'm all right. The injury's gone."

Robbie glanced at the doctor, who was shaking his head in disbelief. "It sounds crazy, but he's right," Emmett said. "The wound is gone."

"He can heal himself most of the time," Cariss said. She hadn't stirred a finger when Duke had been shot. "Whatever is inside him simply absorbs the wound and the pain."

"You'll never cease to amaze me, Duke," Dr. Emmett said as Robbie helped the man up.

Parker came up to them. "Come inside, everyone. We've got to find a way to help these people."

Duke nodded. His eyes had returned to their normal state of warm coals. "Before we go in, I want to apologize. I threw a bit of a fit." He gazed at the ground. "I'm afraid I did not help much by turning into a monster."

"Forget it, Duke," Cariss said blandly.

Parker gave him a lopsided smile. "We forgive you, Duke,

and in the future we'll think up ways to control that side of you."

He smiled back at her. "Thank you, Parker."

Their eyes met and he stared entranced for a moment, until Robbie broke the magic by clearing his throat loudly. "Let's head in," he said.

Emmett nodded. "Jett needs your help in there, Duke. He did a brave thing just now by taking control of things before a fight broke out, but he doesn't know this century as well as you do, and I know he's a reluctant leader."

They made their way inside. In the computer room of the Communications Center, they found Jett, Anton, Ivan and the Rekans. They were finding seats around the tables. Duke took a chair by the main desk and turned it to face the group. Jett sat on one side of him, while Cariss sat at the other. Dr. Emmett sat in a corner with his arms folded, while Robbie and Parker watched from the doorway.

Ivan stood up and cleared his throat. Everyone quieted. "Zank you for offering to help us," he began. "Let me update you on our condition. Zis planet has been in a great food famine for monfs, ever since our crops failed and our livestock died."

"We were never agriculture-based, anyway," another man broke in. "Zis planet provides very little. We have always been heavily dependent on supplies shipped in."

"Yes, zat is true," Ivan agreed.

"How many people live here?" Duke asked.

"We are a colony built around mining, so we have ze miners, and also an outpost of military, our government, and our scientists. Zere are also civilians. All in all, we have about five zousand people."

"Robbie, what is your ship's storage capacity?"

Robbie folded his arms and shook his head. "I'm sorry, Duke, but if we stuffed the *Starlight* full of food over and over again, it wouldn't be enough to make much of a difference."

"But we can still save somebody," Parker persisted.

Ivan fidgeted. "I am afraid you cannot help as much as you zink you can. As you came in, our Sur Liedr Johnson ordered a man to sabotage your ship."

Robbie's eyes widened. "*Starlight?* You sabotaged her? Mark my words and you mark them well! If I ever run into your Sur Leedy again, he's gonna wish with all the fibers of his being that I leave him with, that he'd picked a different ship to mess with!"

"Robbie, hush," Duke said. "Ivan, you say there are five thousand people on this planet who haven't had an actual food supply for months. Is the *Kenswick* trying to bring you some? We saw them outside the force field."

"Yes, it is a freighter sent to bring us supplies. Zey have plenty of food. But zey cannot get past ze force field! Nobody can. Ze people have been starving; ze cities have no more food. We have had several deaths already."

"Is there any food left here at Base?"

Ivan shook his head. "No, zere isn't."

"Yes, zere is," one of the men piped up. He ignored Ivan's glare and continued. "Johnson ordered us to tell ze citizens of Madsville and Kingston we were out. We can save ze important people, he said, if we let some of ze ozers die."

Jett closed his eyes and bowed his head. Teddy wouldn't say a twisted thing like that. He would've found a more heroic thing to say, like *we'll work our hardest to save them all*, not this blatant disregard for others.

"Ze towns are all dying," the man continued quietly. "Zey eizer starve in zeir homes, or freeze outside in zeir search for food. It does not matter anymore, what Johnson said. Zere is no hope for any of us."

12

Force Field

"I can see that things are serious," Duke said, "But something doesn't make sense. Why don't you shut down the force field?"

"We cannot," Ivan said.

Duke waited for an explanation. If there were crickets on Reka, that would have been all he heard. As it was there was total silence. He stood up. "Right now, only a force field stands between you and the death of this entire planet. You set it up, so surely you should know how to turn it off. I ask why you don't shut it down and you say *you can't*?"

"Zere is anozer planet orbiting zis star," one of the men said in a husky whisper. "Reka I. It is merely a rock. Zere is no vegetation on zat planet, no life at all. But it has a breathable atmosphere. Ze force field is around our entire system, keeping bof of our planets shut and locked. In order to shut it off, you must go to ze controls on ze Red Planet."

"How do you get there?" Duke asked.

"Ze Space Agency gave us a transporter. It is a little

sketchy, but we can beam people one at a time from zis planet to ze ozer one wifout ze force field getting in ze way."

"Is the transporter not working?"

"No, it is working."

The Rekans were all sitting deathly still, clutching their chairs and staring holes into the floor. "For goodness' sake, why don't you beam over there?" Duke demanded.

"Ze planet!" one of the men looked up, unearthly fear in his eyes. "Ze planet, it is alive!"

"Alive?" Duke repeated.

The man nodded vigorously. "It will not let us return. It does not want us zere. Ze ground, ze very *ground* rose up and swallowed ze last men we sent zere. I was lucky to escape alive; I was zere. Ze planet ate zem!"

"And it turns men to stone," Ivan said in a low tone, drawing at his pipe. "Ze wind blows, ze dust gets into your eyes, your skin starts to itch, it starts to harden. Wif my own eyes I have watched my comrades turn into statues of red rock."

"No one dares to return to ze planet," a man said. "We would prefer to die here. Starving, at least, is a death we can understand."

A hush fell upon the group. The Rekans sat fidgeting in their chairs, keeping their eyes to the floor. Parker and Robbie were staring with looks of horror. Jett watched Duke, and Dr. Emmett watched Jett.

Duke sank back into his chair. "I'm going over," he decided. "I can't ask any of you to come with me, but I'm going to help these people."

Parker forced the fear on her face aside. "I'm coming," she said. "I came to help you, Duke. I'm sticking with you."

A slight smile crossed his face. "Thank you."

"Don't forget me," said Robbie. "I'm next to useless without the *Starlight*, but I'm willing to do all I can."

"I'm coming too," Jett said. "Teddy set up that force field and he needs it down. I know we came here to arrest him, but... I feel I owe him something."

"Cariss, do you think you could stay here and keep in contact with us, and send us any useful data you can find?" Duke asked.

Cariss turned to the computer behind her, pushing a Rekan out of her way. "I'll track your position on the planet. If you lend me your watch, we'll have better equipment than the Rekans had, and I'll try to warn you against danger."

"And I'll go wherever you need me," Dr. Emmett said.

"Could you stay here and keep an eye out for Tate?" Jett asked.

"And Johnson," Duke added.

Dr. Emmett nodded. "Of course. Please, stay safe." He grasped Jett's and Duke's hands in turn, and Parker gave him a hug. It suddenly dawned on Jett that people had actually died on Reka I. He might never shake hands with the doctor again, or any other Emmett, or King, or Mitchell, or anybody from Nebraska. Logan would never know what had happened to his father. A strong desire began to grow inside Jett, a desire to live. But not for himself. He had been through enough in his life to no longer be selfish. He wanted to live for others. Only in life could he catch crawdads with Logan, or listen to Tate's theories, or search out the paradox twin.

Ivan and several other Rekans led them out of the computer room and into the transporter room. "Stand on ze transporter pad, one at a time," he said. "If all goes well you will arrive on ze Red Planet in one piece."

Dr. Emmett had followed them into the room, and Jett could tell by his face that he was glad he wasn't going. "I'd like to stay in one piece," he heard him mutter.

"It's not that bad," said Robbie, who had also heard him. "Just imagine being disassembled atom by atom and then translated into an electromagnetic wave, and then having your atoms vomited up on the other side."

"Zat is not how zis works," Ivan objected.

"That's how I imagine it," Robbie said.

Duke stepped onto the pad. "Robbie, hush. I'll go first. I've done this before on similar equipment."

"I am ze operator," one of the men said, taking his place behind a control panel. "But zis is madness. Ze planet will swallow you up. It is alive."

"Would you rather us give up?" Jett asked bluntly. "I know you'd prefer to sit here and starve to death, but if I'm going to die, I'm not going to go without a fight."

Ivan shook his head. "It is one zing to die fighting," he said. "It is anozer zing to die in a corner, in terror."

"Are you ready?" asked the operator.

"Wait!" Duke said. "Now that I've had a moment to think about this, I think we need a change of plans. Perhaps I should go alone."

"Are you trying to leave us behind?" Parker said indignantly.

"I have a much better chance of surviving this than any of you," Duke said. "And Parker, what would your family say if something happened to you? You three will be missed. I won't."

"Not to get sentimental, but I'd miss ya," Robbie said. "As they say in all the good stories: we go together or not at all."

"We're coming," Parker said firmly.

"The more minds we have on this problem, the better," Jett said.

"All right," said Duke. He turned to the operator. "I'm ready."

There was a bright flash and Duke was gone. Teleportation, like warp, was another thing Jett didn't understand, and his ignorance actually gave him courage, or something like it. He stepped onto the transporter pad. Before being beamed from one planet to another, he gave a final glance towards Dr. Emmett. Warm, familiar, and never changing: the doctor was the very embodiment of Angel, Nebraska. To Jett, Dr. Emmett was the last link to a former reality, like the last flicker of light in a dark room.

Outside the Communications Center, west from the lake, and partway up a mountain spur, Johnson staggered into his cabin. Duke's pistol had been set to the lowest intensity, so Johnson's wound was a mere burn; but the fall down the stairs had been painful. The walk from Base to his cabin had never been so agonizing. Without even closing the door he limped in and fell onto the floor.

"Jesse," he moaned aloud, feverishly. "Jesse, I'm sorry. I put the force field up to protect myself. I've killed my planet, my dream. I wanted you to live here. You and Logan. And Maddie. I would've brought her back."

"Let me help you," someone said.

Johnson's heart began to beat wildly. He had thought he was alone. With all the energy he had left, he lifted his face off the floor. Outside, the setting sun reflected off the snow, sending rays of light upwards and outlining a figure in the doorway. Johnson squinted, trying to make sense of the silhouette.

"Myshka," he breathed. He moistened his cold, dry lips with his tongue. "Myshka, help me."

The figure stepped in and shut the door. Johnson blinked and stared in the sudden darkness. The person spoke. "I'm not Myshka, but I'll help you."

"Myshka," Johnson said weakly. He decided that he must've hit his head harder than he'd thought, as he could distinctly hear Anton's voice. "Thank you for what you did. You saved me. We'll get through this, I swear."

The figure knelt beside him and laid a hand on his shoulder. "My name is Tate," he said quietly. "I'm Thomas Emmett. You know me."

The realization struck Johnson like a thunderbolt. "Thomas," he gasped. "I left you in Angel in the wrong time, and you got adopted by some relative of Jett's. Sophie, or Sandra, or something."

"Sophie Emmett, yes," Thomas said. He grabbed him by the shoulders and began dragging him across the floor.

"Leave me," Johnson moaned. "Leave me to die. Jesse King

has betrayed me. Anton has deserted me. Madsville is dead. They're dead!"

"Oh stop it!" Tate let go and Johnson's head hit the floor. "I know when a patient is going to die, and you're nowhere near it. You're barely hurt. A few nicks and scrapes, but you're fine. Get over yourself. I'll have you patched up in a minute."

Johnson gaped at the ceiling, his words caught in his mouth. Slowly he relaxed. "Anton would never speak to me like that," he mused.

"Well, maybe Anton isn't a doctor." Tate grabbed Johnson's arm and helped him onto the bench beneath the window. "You took quite a tumble down those stairs. Nasty stuff, ice."

"The laser didn't hurt me much, did it?"

Tate shook his head. He was running his hands along Johnson's arm, squeezing and pressing. "You gave Duke a burn he'll remember, but he barely hurt you."

Johnson yelled suddenly and jerked away. Tate nodded. "Distal radius fracture," he commented. "This will not feel good."

The words seemed familiar. "I broke this same wrist a few days ago," he said slowly.

"Somebody did an impressive job putting it back together," Tate said as he pulled his coat off. "But of course you had to go ruin their hard work. Tell me about when you first broke it."

"I had gone to the Red Planet again. Sheer desperation. I was driven to it." He shuddered.

Tate was using his pocket knife to cut up his jacket. "What's wrong with the Red Planet?"

"I don't want to speak of it, not now." He groaned. "We're all going to die."

"Skip the drama," said Tate. "What about your wrist?"

"I was trying to escape the planet. Men were dying. Never go there."

"And your wrist? Your doctor wants to know."

Johnson grimaced. "I tumbled down a rocky cliff and then ran into the transporter. That's all, if you want me to skip the story and the whole purpose as to why I went there."

"Right now I'm interested in your medical condition. Jett and Duke will take care of the rest. Who set your bone for you?"

"Anton did it first, and then I went into Base the next day where they used their equipment," Johnson said. "Their tools are far more advanced than those of the 21st century, Tate. I had it practically healed in two days."

"Makes me wonder what they can do in Robbie's time," Tate said thoughtfully.

Johnson shook his head. "Besides their ships, they've gone back to the dark ages."

"Now I remember. You've been just about everywhere," Tate said.

A strong gust of wind shook the cabin. The latch on the door rattled, and the window began to flap back and forth. Tate reached over and shut it.

"A storm is kicking in. They come without any warning here," Johnson shivered.

Tate nodded, peering out the window. "The sun has almost disappeared over the mountain. With all this wind and snow no one will come looking for us in the dark, and we can't go anywhere. We'll be stuck here a while."

"You're a fine enough doctor for me," Johnson said mechanically.

"Good, 'cuz you ain't getting anyone else." Tate took the man's arm. "I'm going to do closed reduction, I've always wanted to try it. My uncle has walked me through it a few times."

"Do you really know what you're doing?" Johnson asked as Tate gripped his wrist.

"Of course," he answered.

Pain shot up Johnson's arm. With a scream he crashed his head against the window to fight away the pain, and then sent a well-aimed kick at Tate's head. Before the collision, his leg was caught in a sturdy grip, stopping it halfway.

"Please don't kick your doctor mid-operation," Tate said, shoving the leg aside. "It makes things so much harder."

"It hurt!"

"I'm not surprised," Tate answered drily.

Johnson's temper flared. "You're going to have to find a better way to do this," he shouted, "because I'll kick you every time, like it or not. I'm in pain, can't you have a little sympathy? You're a doctor, haven't you got any painkiller?"

"Look at the stars," Tate said firmly. "Go on, look at them."

The words echoed in Johnson's head as he turned his gaze to the window. The sky was purple above the mountains, while everywhere else was a dim blue. Snowflakes twirled in the strong wind. And up above, thousands of stars twinkled, far more stars here than you could ever see on Earth.

He was focused entirely on the sky, and only when he

heard Tate whisper, "if it hurts, hit the window, not me," did he realize what was happening. His wrist seemed to crack. A wave of nausea swept over him, and he screamed and hit the window with his free hand. A moment later it was over.

"I'm finished, sir. Although I don't know why I'm calling you sir."

Beads of sweat glistened on Johnson's forehead. He leaned his face against the cold window, listening to the howl of the wind, and panting along to it with pain. "Thank you, Myshka," he murmured.

13

The Voice

Cariss squared her shoulders and studied the computer. "Message from *Domzh*," she said.

"Zat is anozer one of ze towns," Ivan said. He was standing behind Cariss' chair. "In our language, it means Home. What do zey say?"

"'Reporting casualties: Abram Senia, 63; Yuli Adrik, 39; Pavel Yeremae, 6 months,'" Cariss read. "Do they need a response?"

"No," Ivan said. "We have nofing to say."

She shrugged and reached over to open a radio line. "You're on, Duke," she said. "I've connected the computer to the Hiero radio, so I have your coordinates on-screen. The reception is good, so I should be able to hear everything."

"Not zat we want to hear everyzing," Ivan said.

"Hold for a moment, Duke. Another written message, this time from the *Kenswick*," Cariss said. "It reads: *'No success with force field. Will keep trying, not optimistic.'*"

Dr. Emmett was sitting in the corner, watching the Rekan men. They were staring at the floor, defeat written across their gaunt faces. He saw a movement in the corner of his eye; turning to look, he saw Anton Venedict peering in. He thought of Tate, and how he had run after Johnson. Outside, the wind was picking up, beating against the walls and painting the windows with snow.

He stood and walked over to Cariss and Ivan. "Is that a storm I hear out there?"

One of the Rekan men jumped to his feet. "We nearly forgot! It always storms on ze eve."

"Ze eve?" the doctor repeated, subconsciously copying the accent.

"Ze Eve of Founder's Day," said Ivan solemnly, drawing at his pipe. "Ze most esteemed day of our planet is tomorrow. I fear it will be our last."

"You cannot light ze candle wifout ze door's code," Anton spoke up, timidly.

Ivan cast him a glance. "Besides Johnson, ze only person who might know ze code would be you. If you do know it, as Sil Liedr I must order you to unlock it. If we are to die we would all prefer to die wif ze candle burning."

All the men murmured in assent.

"I'll unlock it," Anton said, growing bolder, "But only if someone lends me a car."

All eyes turned towards him. "And why, Anton Venedict, would you need a car?" Ivan asked.

"To get up ze mountain, to ze cabin."

One of the men shrugged. "Let him. What use are our cars to us now?"

Ivan nodded. "Come, boy. Open ze door for us."

They all rose and entered the hallway, leaving Cariss at the computer. Dr. Emmett hurried to catch up to Anton. "Listen, son, is this some sort of strange ritual?" he whispered. He wanted to search for Tate, and was highly exasperated by this distraction.

Before Anton could answer, Ivan stepped between them. "It is normally an annual celebration," he explained. "Over fifty years ago a stranger, named Reka, came out of ze sky and named and claimed zis planet. Wif astounding speed and unheard of cooperation from ze Alliance's Space Agency, he founded a colony on zis planet. We were not yet born or merely children on Earf at zat time. But we have heard ze legends of how wifout any funding, he created a solid Base and multiple towns. People flocked to join ze colony."

"Historians say zat what ze Founder did is impossible," another man piped up. "It is our proud heritage: Reka II, ze impossible planet."

"Yes," Ivan said, in almost a question-like way, as if he knew much more than he was letting on.

Dr. Emmett also had suspicions. "And what did you say was the Founder's name?"

"Reka, of course," the man said.

"I believe according to legend," Ivan said, looking at Emmett pointedly, "His full name was Teddy Reka."

"Oh!" the doctor lifted his eyebrows. "And how long has Mr. Johnson been president, may I ask?"

"Four years," Ivan smirked. "I do not know where he was before zat."

They came to a halt outside a locked door. All conversation ceased, and the Rekan men sunk back into their quiet resignation. Anton put four numbers into the combination lock, and then solemnly they marched into the dark room, like a funeral procession; they lined up against the walls, giving everyone a view of the center of the room, where a small table stood. The room was small, and the tight circle of tired men, their eyes sunken and their beards overgrown, made it seem smaller.

The back of Emmett's head brushed against a frame on the wall. There were countless pictures hung up, but in the dark the doctor could not tell what any of them were. Ivan closed the door and the darkness grew deeper. For a few moments there was no sound besides quiet breathing.

"Every year," came Ivan's voice from the blackness, "Ze leaders and elders light zis candle on ze eve, and let it burn until ze new year of new hope. When ze sun rises ze people celebrate outside zese doors. But zis time ze streets will be empty. It is no longer ze beginning of a new year, nor a day of hope. We light zis candle to remember ze dead."

He struck a match. It reflected and glittered in a circle of watching eyes.

"We light zis candle to remember ze years we have been here, ze joys we have had, ze trials. We light zis candle today, and it will burn into ze end of ze age, ze last days of Reka. It shall burn until zere is nofing left to burn for: in days to come, we shall watch it as we die. Ze flame shall die wif Reka."

The match touched the candle. The flame caught and flickered, and the wax began to soften. "Let us have a moment of silence for our colony, which has perished beneath undeserved woes."

The words had hardly left his mouth when, either by some trick of the candle, or a movement from one of the men, the flame went out. The darkness consumed them, and the silence that followed was deeper and blacker than the darkness itself. A shiver ran down Emmett's spine. And then suddenly, one of the men gave a shriek of despair.

The cry shook its hearers to the very marrow of their bones, and Emmett broke into a cold sweat. Fumbling with the matches, Ivan lit the candle again, casting a dim light over the room. There was no way of knowing who had given the shriek; the doctor glanced about at their strained, pale faces, and knew it could have been any one of them. "Let us resume our silence," Ivan said, putting emphasis on the last word.

Dr. Emmett cleared his throat. "If it's all the same to you," he said, "Anton and I are going for a little drive."

"You do not want to join us in our last moments?"

"I'm more concerned about saving lives than grieving them right now," Emmett answered. "I'll skip the drama. Let's go, Anton."

He felt around for the door, and Anton slipped out with him before Ivan could restrain him. They walked down the hallway, and Dr. Emmett blinked as his eyes adjusted to the light.

"You are going to ze cabin too?" Anton asked.

"Of course. You're worried about Johnson, I'm worried about Tate."

Anton stared at the floor. "Ze road is dangerous wif ze snow. Perhaps it would be better sir, if you stay here."

Dr. Emmett snorted. "And join the mourning party? Where there's life, there's hope, though it seems these people would rather waste away their time. It feels as if they're bury-ing their colony in there."

"Zey are," Anton said. "Ze *Kenswick* cannot get in, ze *Starlight* cannot get out, and ze food is gone. Zey say a hundred people in Kingstown and Madsville have died. Ze people of Domzh are dying, did you not hear? I used to live in Domzh." His voice trembled.

"I'm sorry, Anton," the doctor said. "I guess that throughout all of Time there will always be people who suffer much more than folks in Nebraska could ever imagine. I'm beginning to realize how blessed I've been. I'll try to be more sympathetic."

"It does not matter," Anton said. "Zere is no hope."

The hallway ended, and they paused before the door that would lead them into the dark outer world. Dr. Emmett looked at the young Rekan. Anton was short for his age, and the famine had left him thin and wasted like the others. His eyes were glossy with tears that had never been shed; they shone like blue diamonds in his face of white sand. His accent, his language, his home and his moods were unfamiliar and tragic, but somehow, beneath his crop of curly hair, there was a boy Dr. Emmett knew.

He laid his hand on Anton's shoulder, and though the boy trembled he stood his ground. "Well, son," he said kindly, "I don't know about there not being any hope. There's always hope, as long as we're willing to look for it. Strangely enough, it's rare to find someone who is. That's one thing that's the same in my day as yours."

"We must hurry, sir," Anton said, side-glancing at the door.

"Wait a moment," the doctor said. "I've got a rather

strange question for you. Do you ever feel as if you're connected to someone?"

"Ze Voice? Ze Mirror?" Anton said slowly.

"You're the paradox twin! Did you see my nephew Tate? You pick up on his thoughts and feelings sometimes, don't you?"

"I do not pay attention."

"I bet it was that Johnson who told you to ignore it," Emmett said. "You Rekans are as tight as clams (unless you're talking about the end of the world), but feel free to say what you'd like around me. I want to know who you are and how you ended up out here. You can tell me anything; Tate always does."

"But I am not Tate."

"In a way, you are!" Dr. Emmett insisted. "You're a lot thinner, you've got more hair, and your clothes are better fitted for the weather, but you're his twin nonetheless, and you've got a stronger connection than any twin before you. Your minds fit together perfectly, ignoring every other rule of the universe. You're completely identical in looks, too, though I think you may be younger than him right now. Can you feel anything from him at the moment?"

"Do not make me speak of ze Voice!" Anton said. He was shaking, but he kept his eyes locked with Emmett's. "Sur Liedr needs me to look for him. Sur Liedr is more important zan ze Voice."

"Sur Liedr is Johnson?" Emmett said, as a statement rather than a question. "It's always Johnson with you, isn't it? He'd better appreciate your help and loyalty."

"I do not always do zings well," Anton said, and his eyes dropped to the floor.

"I noticed something earlier," Dr. Emmett said, changing the subject slightly. He pushed up Anton's sleeve and ran a finger over a long, dark scar. "What is that from?"

"Zat is from a bad day."

Emmett's face darkened. "Who had the bad day, you or Johnson?"

Anton looked at him drily. "I zink ze bof of us, sir."

Dr. Emmett shook his head. "Sometimes you speak, and I hear Tate talking."

"I am sorry, sir."

"No, don't be sorry," Emmett said. "And I'm sorry for asking about it, but I'm a doctor so I can't help but notice things."

"May we go now, sir?"

"I'm ready," the doctor answered. "And I hope you know, son, that when this is all over you can always find friends in Tate and me, and even a home if need be."

"Zis will not end ze way you zink it will," Anton said.

He spoke with an emptiness and a hopelessness that was strange coming from someone so young. Emmett searched his mind, desperately trying to think of something to say to encourage him. Reka had fallen into a despair of utter blackness, and Anton had been lost along with it. They opened the door, exposing themselves to the cold, windy night.

"My friends are out there," Dr. Emmett said as they went out, more to himself than Anton. "And I think they're willing to keep trying, no matter how dark things get."

14

The Red Planet

On Reka I, Duke, Jett, Robbie and Parker stood in the transporter building. This was where they had found themselves after beaming in from Reka II. There was not much in the building, beside the transporter pads, a bucket of picks and rock-cutting equipment, and a door leading outside. Jett could not find a window, so as of yet he had little idea of what the planet looked like.

"Are you back, Cariss?" Duke asked the radio.

"Yes, apologies," she answered. "I had to find Ivan and bring him back here. He had left for some Founders Eve ceremony. I'm looking over the information on this computer, and it appears that it's a bit of a walk to the force field controls. There are two trails: you will see them both when you step out of the building."

"Which is faster?"

"Bof of zem are difficult," came Ivan's voice. "Bridges, stairs, and zings like zat are unfinished. We were still working on zem when ze planet came to life. Bof trails are about ze same length, and zey bof lead to ze caverns where ze controls are kept."

"Caverns?" Robbie said, uncertain. "This just got a lot more exciting."

"You were warned," said Ivan gravely. "No man in zeir right mind would attempt zis. No man in zeir right mind."

Duke clipped the Hiero radio to his belt. "Let's head outside," he said. They nodded in agreement, and Jett opened the door. The four of them stepped out.

The planet was eerily still. Low mountains and cliffs hung above them in every direction, all a dark red color. The sky was gray, stained with red. The crags were red. The dusty ground beneath their feet was red. The planet was carved from rock: no dirt, no vegetation, and no other color but a copper red.

"By *two trails*," Jett said tentatively, "Did Cariss mean *that?*"

The rock face immediately before them was broken in two places, and small cracks, like doorways, led into the mountains.

"I'm glad it's daytime on this side of the planet," Robbie said, stuffing his hands into his pockets and trying to smile. "This would be pure torture in the dark."

"We won't have daylight for long," Duke noted in concern, gazing at the black shadow on the horizon. "It would be more efficient if we split up. Is that alright with all of you?"

Parker nodded bravely. "Whatever you say, Duke."

"How about Parker and I to the right, and Robbie and Jett to the left."

They split into pairs and approached the two entrances.

Casting each other final glances, they disappeared into the doorways.

Jett heard Robbie give a sigh of relief. "This isn't so bad. It looks like a wretched hole from the outside, but I can see the sky. Mountain's sorta close on both sides, though."

They had found themselves in a hallway of rock. Far up above them rose the towering cliff walls, and above that the red sky. Jett felt claustrophobic. He reached out with both of his arms, and found he could touch the two sides with his fingertips.

"The planet seems rather dead to me," Jett heard Robbie continue, his voice echoing. "No arms, no eyes. Nothing creepy. Although it is sort of like being shut up in a box. If the sky wasn't the same color as the rock it wouldn't be so bad, but it gives you the feeling of being swallowed alive."

"Can't you be quiet?" Jett hissed. Though he was whispering, his voice still echoed. "We've got to hurry and reach the force field controls before we really are swallowed alive."

"I don't like the quiet," Robbie groaned. "But I'll stop if you want me to."

After a few minutes of silence, Jett began to wonder if letting Robbie talk hadn't been the brighter idea. The planet was still, too still; the pathway was endless. His feet were beginning to drag and his arms weighed him down like bags of sand. The quiet was stifling. He began longing for the splashing of water, a chirping bird, or a friendly voice.

"Do you think this is really one of the trails?" Robbie whispered at length. "I've got a Hiero, but do you think Cariss is tracking ours or only Duke's? Perhaps the trails were at the other side of the transporter room, east and not west. This could be an endless canyon going clear across the planet. The air is really still here. Oh man, I'd do anything for a bit of wind!"

Jett stopped and Robbie crashed into him. Pushing him off he asked in a hushed voice, "Is it just me, or are the walls closer?"

Robbie began stretching his arms out and his hands bumped against the walls. He pressed both forearms against either side. "It's getting tighter."

Jett looked up. The sky had merged with the cliffs in a steady, deep red. They truly were in a box.

"Call Cariss," he said. "We'd better make sure she knows we split up."

"We never did a soundcheck with this radio, only Duke's," Robbie said worriedly. "What if this one doesn't work?"

"I'm sure it'll work, just do it!"

Robbie pulled the radio off his belt. "Cariss? Anyone?"

"Cariss here."

"Are we going the right direction?" Jett asked.

"Yes, I'm tracking your position," she said. "According to this computer, you should be in the cavern by now, or very close."

Robbie's eyes brightened. "Not too much farther now! You know, Cariss, if you have Duke's watch you can track us with more accuracy. I helped him put on a new feature that allows you to track the latitude, longitude, and elevation of his Hiero radios. If you can manage to turn it on, you'll be able to see if we've dropped in elevation, meaning we've gone down into a cavern..."

"Robbie, shh." Jett frowned and his eyes darted back and forth. "Robbie, the walls! We haven't been moving."

Robbie lifted his arms and immediately his hands hit rock. Visions of being flattened between cliffs raced through Jett's mind as he watched him push against the walls. They were nearly touching his shoulders.

"Perhaps I'm dreaming," Robbie said.

"You really don't like tight spaces, do you?"

Robbie swallowed and shook his head. "Nobody likes getting sandwiched."

Jett nodded, his eyes alert and his jaw tense. "Let's keep moving."

Suddenly a groan erupted, echoing through the passage, growing louder and louder. It was a rumbling groan of rock on rock. In a flash the trail disappeared behind them. The walls grabbed Robbie's shoulders.

"Run!" Jett shouted, dashing forwards.

The two men sprinted down the rapidly closing passage. The silence was broken. The mountain was heaving, and the rock faces swung towards them as if trying to bite. The sky disappeared and was replaced by rock. Jett crashed into a hard corner and Robbie collided with him. There was red rock above, beneath, around; they were trapped in a rapidly diminishing bubble.

"Call Cariss!" Jett screamed.

The mountain screeched and groaned. Jett felt his ribs and back being pinched closer together and his heart was pumping against solid rock. Robbie fumbled with the radio, and dropped it. The walls swallowed it and it disappeared.

Jett groped above his head, and felt the rock closing about his fingers. Robbie was pushed against him.

"You were warned," moaned Robbie, mimicking Ivan's accent. "No man in zeir right mind would attempt zis. No man in zeir right mind!"

15

Parker's Future

"How good are you at rock climbing?" Duke asked.

"Never tried it, but I'm game," answered Parker.

Johnson and his men had chiselled small steps into the steep rock face, and a rope hung down to help with traction and balance. Duke grabbed hold of it and pulled. It was sturdy, and he guessed it had been used before safely. He placed a foot on the first step and nearly slid off.

"This rock is slippery," he muttered, trying again and leaning more heavily on the rope. "Make sure you keep a tight hold with your hands."

He began climbing, shooting occasional glances below him to check on Parker. She was keeping up perfectly. About halfway to the crest his eyes caught a glimpse of color beside his hand. Beside the copper red of the rock, he hadn't seen any color on this planet, so he frowned and leaned closer. Growing out of the rock was a fragile, purple flower.

His first thought was how beautiful it would look in Parker's blond hair, or even just her hand. He reached for it and touched it. It gave him a static shock and he pulled his hand away quickly. If it looked too good to be true, he decided, it probably was. Leaving it there, he turned his eyes up towards the red rock and red sky.

A few moments later he heard Parker give a slight cry. His heart froze. He glanced down and saw her clutching the rope, trying to smile. "Sorry," she said. "I slipped a little, that's all."

"You scared me! Don't let go of the rope, do you hear? Both hands!"

She smiled. "Got it!"

After a few more minutes, they reached the top. Cariss' voice came over the Hiero radio on Duke's belt.

"I'm picking up a terrible disturbance," she said. "I've been running tests on it. It's some kind of windstorm."

"Windstorm?" Duke eyed the horizon. It was hard to interpret the weather. On one side, the sky met the ground in a rusty red, while on the other there was the blackness of oncoming night. "How bad of a storm?"

"Winds strong enough to slam you against ze wall and break your neck," came Ivan's voice. "Anozer reason we avoid ze planet now."

"According to this data, I must agree with his description," Cariss said. "According to my calculations, if this storm reaches the transporter building, it will demolish it in a manner of seconds, and you'll have no way out."

"Look at our position on your computer," Duke said. "Are we at least close to the controls?"

They heard Ivan gasp. "You are not dead? Zis is unheard of. Ze cavern is to your left. You must hurry before you run into trouble."

"But you won't have enough time to get back to the transporter unless you rush over *now*," Cariss said, "And that's your only way off this planet. We'll beam you up. Let me find Robert's signal…"

Her voice trailed off. Duke listened, growing more anxious as the silence went on. At length she spoke again, low and serious. "Their signal has disappeared. That entire area is covered by the storm. I recommend you run for your lives."

Parker's eyes widened and she glanced at Duke. His determination wavered, but then his face set. "I've got to shut down that force field."

"It's plain suicide now. If you come back we can fix Robbie's spaceship, and at least a few of us will be able to get out."

"But what about us?" Ivan exclaimed.

"And what about Madsville? From what I heard, the people there died because you'd rather save yourself than the women and children," Duke reminded. He shook his head and sighed. "Do you deserve to live, Ivan? You've killed your neighbors to save yourself. After your selfishness you deserve nothing more than to die of starvation."

There was a heavy moment of silence. Duke sighed again. "Cariss, keep tracking us. The cavern is to the left?"

"You are saving us," said Ivan, his voice full of disbelief. "But why?"

"Mercy, I guess. I'm giving you another chance."

"Turn left at a hundred yards," Cariss directed.

Duke and Parker headed in that direction. They were on a sort of plateau or mesa. The wind flitted about them, tossing red sand between their feet and through their fingers. Parker folded her arms and hunched forward to protect her face from the wind, but as she did so she felt something cold against her arm.

She glanced down, but there was nothing. Her fingers might be cold, she decided. She splayed them out in front of her and her heart skipped a beat. The tips of her right hand had turned a rusty red. She touched it and it was hard. She squeezed it, pinched it, and tried to pull it off, but to no avail. Her fingers were turning into the same red rock as the mountain she stood on.

"Park, are you coming?"

She looked up and saw Duke's warm eyes watching her. She shivered, clutching her hand against her heart. "Yes, I'm coming."

She followed him to the mouth of a cave, opening up in the ground. Rough, chiselled stairs led into the dark hole. Duke held out his hand to help her down, but she avoided it. "I can go down myself," she said. "I'm fine, really." She avoided his eyes and began the descent. Her voice echoed as she continued talking. "I'm really proud of you, Duke. For saving Reka, I mean."

"You're still with me," Duke said, stepping in behind her. "I'm not doing anything more than you."

He touched the walls. They were cold; the temperature was dropping. He unclipped the Hiero from his belt and flipped on the built-in light.

"This passage winds down a little ways," Parker observed.

Duke skipped a couple steps to catch up with her and began walking by her side. "I don't like the look of this cave. I wish there were puddles, or dripping noises. There is absolutely nothing on this planet but rock." He shook his head. "I shouldn't have let you all come. You must be terrified."

"I'm not terrified," she said. "I'm sad for Robbie and Jett but I'm not scared. Rock doesn't scare me. At least not in mountains and caves. Can I see the Hiero?"

"So it's the dark that scares you?" Duke asked. He felt her hand touch his as she took the Hiero, and for a moment his heart warmed. But then it skipped a beat as Parker turned the light towards herself. Her entire right hand was a rusty red.

"It started on my fingertips," she said with her lop-sided smile which now seemed eerily out of place. "But then it spread. There are streaks of it up my wrist." The light was pointed at her hand, but it dimly illuminated her eyes, teeth, and strands of blond, untidy hair, and cast her creeping shadow against the dark wall.

"Can you move your fingers?"

She shook her head. "It's solid rock, Duke. I'm turning into rock!"

He reached out a hand and guided the Hiero away, obscuring the horrible sight with darkness. She looked up into his face; his eyes glowed as flames of sympathy. "Let's hurry," he whispered. "I'll find a way to rush you back to the transporter. Cariss and Dr. Emmett can find a way to save you."

"How do you save a rock?" she cried, bordering hysteria. "I'm going to die here with Jett and Robbie and there's nothing we can do about it!"

"You are not going to die," he said. "There may be a way to survive, but we've got to find it!"

She sobbed and turned away.

Duke grabbed her shoulder. "Say it: no one else will die to-day."

Parker sobbed, but her tear-stained face set with determination. "No one else will die today."

He grabbed her hand and pulled her down the passage. "Let's go save Reka."

And so they ran. The storm above them grew, but they felt none of it in the deep hallways of the cave. As they ran, Duke's mind began to wander. Though an entire colony was depending on him, and his own life was at risk, he found he could think of nothing but the blond girl beside him, her hand in his. He thought of bringing her home safely, of visiting her childhood home in Georgia. He scolded himself mentally, and tried everything he could to distract himself, from imagining dying of starvation to reciting the multiplication table. But his thoughts could not be severed from Parker Quinn.

After several minutes of running, he was struck with a chilling discovery. Patches of rock were forming on his arms and hands. His blood was running fast, as if trying to fight off the stone that threatened to block his veins.

"It itches!" Parker cried. She scratched at her arm desperately, and red silt fell into her hand. "I can't feel the rock, but where it's still part skin and only beginning to change, it…"

"Keep running," Duke interrupted. "We can do it, Parker. We're almost to the controls."

"At least I've gotten to hear my name before dying," she said. "Everybody but you calls me Quinn. That's what they call me at college, that's what my aunt calls me, that's what Robbie calls me…"

"Parker," Duke said, turning around to face her. "Parker, we've got to hurry."

Suddenly they heard a loud groan.

"What is that?" Parker whispered.

The walls began to creak and shudder.

Instinctively, Duke pulled out his laser pistol. Parker shook her head. "I don't think that'll do much good if the mountain is trying to eat us." She frowned. "Your hands are glowing."

He glanced down. "No, no!" he wailed, flailing his arms. His body tingled and glowed with a transparent fire, and he began to fade from Parker's sight. "I'm shifting out of time again. I'll be back in a moment. Stay there!"

Parker eyed him curiously. She had never seen this happen, but Duke had told her before that he was occasionally thrown into a different time and place. There was nothing he could do to stop it. She began to wonder how it happened, and why, but there was no time for her to ask any questions.

Duke closed his eyes. Last time this had happened, he had found himself in a docking bay in England, 1780 or thereabouts. And he had been *in* the water. He felt his body steady and he dared to open his eyes.

He was no longer on Reka in the 23rd century. Instead, he was standing in a full, bright room. Blue and purple decorations hung from the ceiling and every window. There were nearly a dozen round tables scattered about, each with a white tablecloth and a bouquet of flowers in the middle. The guests were laughing and eating together happily. Nobody seemed to notice him.

He turned and his eyes rested on a long table. His heart went cold. Parker Quinn was decked out in a beautiful white dress. Duke knew that this must be Parker's future, as she had never been married. She stood beaming in front of the wedding clan's table, getting a picture taken with her groom. Duke's palms began to sweat, and his grip on the pistol tightened. Standing beside Parker in a fine black suit was Jesse King.

Somehow, Jett survived Reka I and would end up here. Jealousy burned through his body like fire, and Duke acted without thinking. He flipped his pistol's intensity to the highest setting. A red stream blazed out and hit Jett in the chest and he crumpled. Now Duke had everyone's attention. People screamed; some got up and fled. Out of the corner of his eye he saw Tate Emmett rising from behind the main table, knocking his chair over. He saw Robbie run over from somewhere. And Duke saw his future self, sitting behind the table, his face in his hands.

Parker had dropped to her knees on the floor beside Jett. She looked up, tears in her green eyes. "You killed him," she whispered.

His hands flamed again. Suddenly he was in a black, empty vacuum, far away from the wedding, and then he found himself staring at a red wall. Blinking, he turned and his eyes met Parker's. She was standing in the passageway on Reka I in the 23rd century, right where he had left her a moment before. He had a sudden impulse to blurt out what had happened: he had fallen into their future, and he had murdered Jett. But then Duke was overwhelmed with a surge of guilt, still mingled with rage. There was no way to undo it. Parker and Jett would live to this certain fate.

"You're back," Parker said, awakening him from his thoughts.

"Yes," he answered. "We'd better shut down the force field."

16

Meeting the Miner

As Jett slowly came to his senses, there was nothing but eerie silence, and he wondered if he was dead. He wanted to open his eyes, but he had an intense fear of opening them to nothing but red rock. A heavy weight pressed against his ribcage, sending a panicked message to his brain that he was still being smothered. But strangely, his head and legs felt free. Cautiously he cracked open an eye.

He was almost relieved when he saw pitch black. Anything, he figured, was better than red. He listened for the mountain's groanings, which was the last thing he remembered hearing, but everything was quiet except the sound of his own breathing. One arm was pinned but he could move the other with ease. He reached up and touched a warm, live something lying on top of him.

Jett gave a little yelp and pushed it off. As his hands made contact, he recognized the feel of hair. "Robbie?" he exclaimed, sitting up.

"Jett," the man muttered as he slowly came to his senses. Jett felt around and felt a cold wall behind him; he leaned up against it and tried to relax his taut muscles. Straining his eyes he tried to figure out where he was, but the darkness gave him no clue.

"Robbie, do you have a light?" he whispered, feeling through his pockets.

A small bubble of light appeared, lighting Robbie's face in a dim, blue glow. "It's my watch," he explained. "All I've got, I'm afraid. The Hiero must be smashed."

"Weren't we smashed?"

Robbie scooted up beside him and leaned his back on the wall. "That's what I thought."

Jett staggered to his feet. His legs wobbled like jelly, and something in his stomach was doing somersaults. He put a hand against the wall, and then his head hit the ceiling. Pain fizzed beneath his scalp and behind his eyes.

"Careful standing up," he grunted as he heard Robbie moving beside him. "The ceiling is low, and I'm short."

Suddenly the walls rumbled. In the tiny bubble of light Jett saw Robbie's eyes widen. Without hesitation both men plunged forward blindly, scrambling to get away from the wall.

Jett had barely covered ten feet before his face smashed into another wall. Tumbling into Robbie the two men crashed to the ground. "My watch," Robbie gasped. They were in complete darkness. "I took it off, and you knocked it out of my hand!"

There was another deep groan and the floor beneath them shook. Jett could feel the wall compressing his feet. Desperately he felt the ground for Robbie's watch. His hand bumped into something and he grabbed it.

"The Hiero, Robbie, I found the Hiero!"

"But I was sure it was broken!"

"I don't know how to use it, take it!" Jett felt for Robbie and thrust it into his hand. A second later its bright light sliced through the room. The ceiling was closing down on their heads; the walls were only a few yards apart. They were in a closing grip of red rock. Jett felt his limbs forced against the ground and then he lost consciousness.

Seemingly a moment later, he woke up with a start. By now the hard stone beneath him felt familiar. He sat up, listening for sound and feeling for a wall. It was pitch black again, and the air was thin and had a slight chill.

"Good mornin'," a voice spoke.

Jett jumped in surprise and hit his head against an outcrop of rock. The Voice continued, rough and echoing, as if the rock itself had learned to speak.

"I suppose zis means ze force field is still up? Well, if we're all gonna die anyway, I'm glad I won't die lonely."

The ground rumbled like distant thunder. Jett scraped his fingers against the wall and sweat pricked his neck. The Voice laughed. "Don't even try, stranger. Since I've been down here, I've done what you're doing now. Fallin' down, climbin' up. But zis is ze planet's garbage system, plungin' us deeper and deeper, faster zan anyone could climb out."

"There's a way up?" Jett croaked, his throat scratched and dry with dust.

There was a shrug in the man's voice. "Sure. Once you get your night vision, you can see all sorts of cracks and holes and tunnels opening up all over ze place. But wifout knowin' which crack and hole and tunnel goes where, what's ze point?" He gave a hoarse, desperate laugh that echoed throughout the cavern, sounding more maniacal with each repeat. "But I don't recognize your voice, stranger. You aren't one of us Rekans; I take it you're from the States. Who are you?"

A bright light suddenly shone in Jett's face. He covered his eyes and could just barely see Robbie clutching the Hiero. "My name is Jesse King," he said, searching the shadows for the man. "I'm from Nebraska... the States... Earth. This is my friend Robbie. We heard of the famine and everything and decided to help."

Robbie turned the Hiero towards the corner, revealing the form of a ragged man with torn clothes and mud-matted hair and beard. "Help?" the man repeated. He swore and shook his head. "Reka needed *help* four years ago when zat double-crosser Johnson first came to term. To help, you're far too late."

Jett leaned against the wall and slowly sank into a crouching position. He no longer could hear the groaning. "What do you mean? What did Johnson do?"

"I've lived on that frozen wasteland for twenty years, so mark my words as ones comin' from someone who really knows somethin'," the man said, idly brushing dirt off his knees. "The Alliance was willing to back the Space Agency on their Reka project all zose years ago because of its minerals. Zat's my job; I used to do mining on Earf. And it's all zat planet is good for, in my opinion. Scientists and military outposts, zat's good and proper too. But Johnson wanted a settlement."

He kicked the wall and spat in disgust. His mood seemed to swing between resignation and desperate outbursts. "Settlement, I tell you! Ze man is mad. He wanted families, and cabins, and cars. My people were refugees wifout a home, so of course we jumped on ze chance of having our own planet, but he never told us about ze danger, or ze loneliness, or about how he would be our tyrant. Johnson makes the rules, all of zem!"

He calmed down and folded his arms. A maniacal smile crept onto his face. "But Space is dangerous, and Space has its own rules. These planets have got zeir own ideas of physics. Zat Johnson is a demented old soul who wants to force colonization onto Space, but I tell you, even ze most beautiful, Earf-like planets out here are deadly."

"If it was that obvious that the Red Planet was dangerous, your president would've noticed and done something different, or at least his advisors," Jett reasoned. "All this must've been unexpected."

The man shook his head. "The man is mad, I tell you, and he does not listen to advisors! How he became president I'll never know. He has his own ideas and he doesn't care a zing about safety or lives, unless it's his own that's in the noose. But look where zat landed me!" He fisted the wall. "We told him not to set up ze force field, but he insisted. Now we've got to kill ourselves to shut it off so our families don't die of starvation!"

"Why did he put the force field up?"

"I reckon it was to save his own skin," the man answered grimly. "The way he rules Reka can't be legal. With a force field like ze one he's got, he can keep snooping eyes out and tattletales in. But after zis whole famine thing started, he sent us down here to shut it off while he lingered outside like a coward. Ze men who were wif me have undoubtedly suffocated by now down below. I'm short of breath myself. All because Johnson is lord of all and we do as he says! I'd die gladly if only I first had a chance to get my hands around his neck and..."

The walls began to sway. Jett jumped to his feet. "I would love to talk longer, but we're about to die. How do we get out?"

The man shook his head. "Shine your light around and you'll see cracks and tunnels. Try if you will, but I zink I'll be seein' you again soon. Zere's no way of knowing which direction to go. You'll get lost and run out of air."

"Robert?" Cariss' voice blared over the speaker. "Robert Finley, are you there?"

"I'm here!" he answered.

"Your signal disappeared and we assumed you had died. Where are you? I have your location on screen again, but according to my data you should be in the middle of a windstorm."

The miner lurched to Robbie's side. "Zey can track your signal zrough all this rock?"

The walls began to tremble and reach for each other. Gaping cracks widened on both sides.

The miner's eyes flashed wildly. "Direction! Ask for direction! If zere's a chance to get out of here..."

"Which way am I going, Cariss?" Robbie shouted, rushing towards a crack.

"Towards the transporter. North, in this planet's geography. Are you in immediate danger?"

"Yeah! Just let me know if we change elevation, okay?" Robbie said before stuffing the Hiero into his pants pocket.

A wall hit against Jett's side, momentarily knocking the wind out of him. His stomach rose with pain and fear. Robbie scrambled into the crack, and Jett staggered after him, climbing in on his hands and knees. The miner leapt in behind them, bursting with animation now that he had a clear idea of direction. The ground moved with a grinding roar and the entrance to the tunnel closed up. Jett jerked himself deeper in as the rock swallowed the path behind him. The miner pushed against him frantically, driving him forward.

Jett's mind was swirling with conflicting thoughts of Teddy, but he forced them out and focused on crawling for his life. It was a small tunnel, barely large enough for them to squeeze through. It fluctuated in size and shape, sometimes rounded, sometimes jagged, and it climbed steadily upward. The three men crawled and wormed their way along. The rumbling ceased, and the tunnel went perfectly still. At one point it narrowed and Jett thought his shoulders would crack, but he forced himself through and it widened farther up.

"Watch it, Jett!" Robbie shouted suddenly. "Jett! ...there's a drop-off on this side."

Jett froze. Robbie shone the Hiero to their left, where a deep chasm had opened up. With the strange urge that affects most humans in a situation like this, Jett groped around for a large chunk of red rock and pushed it over. He counted to ten before he heard several crashes, and he imagined the clay-like rock splintering into thousands of pieces.

Robbie was several yards ahead, but he spun around and shone the Hiero behind him when he heard the noise. "Jett?" he said, panicked.

"I'm all right," Jett said, inching forward as the miner caught up with him. "Keep going."

The ground began to vibrate beneath their feet and hands. The surge of panic Jett felt was like an old friend. He staggered onto his feet, and though his head brushed the ceiling and the chasm looked up hungrily at him on his left, he broke into a run.

"There's a higher level up here!" Robbie called back. "Hurry before things close up!"

A heavy hand caught Jett mid-stride. It was the miner, fighting and clawing his way ahead. Jett staggered and pitched head-foremost towards the chasm, catching his chin on the edge with his body sprawled out on the narrow ledge. The miner clambered forward, until a shockwave hit the ground beneath them.

Jett lost track of the miner as the ground threw him over the edge, and he found himself clinging to the ledge with one desperate arm and leg. Somebody screamed, and the countless echoes sent chills through Jett's body. Hands grabbed his shoulders, and he tensed, fearing the shove of the miner. But the hands jerked him onto the ground, and looking up he found Robbie hovering over him. "Come on!" he shouted, grabbing him and dragging him along.

Jett staggered to his feet to keep his friend from dislocating his arm. Keeping a firm grip on his wrist, Robbie pulled him into the gap leading to the higher level. They tumbled out the other side, and Jett fell face-first on the ground. The tunnel grinding shut behind them, Jett lay still, hugging the cold floor. The groanings ceased, and all was quiet except for his and Robbie's jagged breaths.

"The... miner?" Jett panted, too exhausted and drained by adrenaline to elaborate on his question.

"Lost his balance. Went over the edge." Robbie rolled onto his back. "I looked back and you both were gone." He shuddered.

"Thanks, man." Jett didn't know what else to say. After a minute had passed by, he supported himself on his forearms. "The Hiero... shine it around."

With a shaky nod Robbie sat up and turned on the radio's light. They were in a large, airy cavern, and though it was made of the same red rock it hardly reminded Jett of the claustrophobic spaces they had been in. The ceiling was high, joining smoothly with the walls, giving a rounded look to the room. At one place there was an arched crack leading out, resembling a doorway.

"Are you all right, Robbie?" Jett asked. With no immediate danger in sight, he rolled onto his back and took a deep breath.

"I think so." His voice was unsteady. "How does all this work? Why aren't we dead?"

Jett glanced over. The radio was perfectly intact, without so much as a dent, and besides a few cuts and scrapes Robbie was in one piece as well. "We were dragged down to a lower level, or something. That's what the miner said." He shuddered as he remembered the scream, and a feeling of nausea overtook him.

"So the planet *did* eat us. We just crawled out of its stomach, or something," Robbie said.

"The miner said that this planet has its own laws of physics. It's like an organic transporter."

"There's nothing organic about this, Jett. It's a pure nightmare." Robbie shivered. "Are we going to be stuck down here forever, trying to climb out its throat? What if it sends us down faster than we can climb up? We've fallen into this planet's waste system!"

"We'll make it, Robbie," Jett said resolutely. "If you want to give up I'm sure the planet will appreciate the company. But if you stick with me, we're getting out of here. Cariss is tracking us, remember? She knows how deep we are too, like you said. Call her."

Robbie pressed down a button. "Robbie here. Can you hear me still?"

The radio crackled. "I lost your signal again for a moment. Wherever you are, it's hard to track you. What's wrong?"

"Oh, not much," he answered, "Besides the fact that we're far out of our correct time periods in an attempt to save a frozen wasteland from starvation and we've been stranded on a desert planet that's trying to eat us!"

"Robert, you are truly about to be stranded. A storm is blowing in that will destroy the transporter building, which is your only way out."

He bashed his fist against the wall. "And the *Starlight* is sabotaged! We never even caught Johnson!"

"I can give you directions to get back to the transporter.

Duke's still trying to shut off the force field, but after that he'll be stuck there. But you've got a chance to save yourselves."

Jett took the Hiero. "Could you help us navigate to join up with him?"

"You don't intend to come back?" she asked.

"Not quite yet. If something happens to Duke, it's up to us to shut off that force field," he answered.

"It takes a little more than a planet-wide garbage disposal to stop us," Robbie agreed.

"I thought that would be your decision," Cariss said, cool and even as usual, giving no indication of whether she approved of it or not. "You're very close to the force field controls. You must steer a course east."

The two men glanced about at the red rock. "East?" repeated Jett. "Which way is that?

"Begin walking," she said. "I'll inform you as to whether it's the right direction, and if you're progressing up or down."

17

Reunion

Duke and Parker dashed down the rock corridor, their Hi-ero lighting up the red walls, red floors, and red ceiling. All of a sudden they reached an abrupt edge. A narrow chasm lay between them and the next stretch of the passage. On the ground beside them, there were long metal slats and crates full of materials and equipment for building a bridge, but as it was unmade, Johnson and his men had strung up a rope to swing from one side to another. It was not a wide gap by any means, and Duke figured he could jump across even without the rope's aid.

"I can't jump that," Parker moaned, sinking to her knees. "Go on, Duke. You've gotta shut off the force field."

"I'm not leaving you here!" Duke objected. "I'll carry you across."

Parker shook her head. "Don't be foolish, Duke. I'm only slowing you down. Get over there and find the controls!"

Duke stalled, torn between his better judgment and his protective feeling of Parker. At length he nodded. "I'll be back. The controls should be close. I'll be as quick as I can."

He took a running jump and landed on the other side of the gap. Parker watched him turn a final glance in her direction, and then he disappeared around the corner. She clutched her arm with her good hand and backed against the wall, stifling a sob. Never before had she felt so alone. Adrenaline coursed through her, keeping her tense and panting. She felt it was impossible to stand there and do nothing, but it was growing harder to move, rendering it impossible for her to do anything else. There was nothing to look at, think of, or feel, except for the red rock of the planet that was slowly creeping through her veins.

She heard footsteps behind her, and then Jett and Robbie appeared from around the corner. Both of their faces broke into uncontrollable smiles when they saw her, and Robbie laughed with sheer joy. Tears blurred Parker's vision, and she found herself laughing too. "You're alive!" she sobbed. "I thought you were dead!"

"Where's Duke?" Robbie asked.

She gestured towards the ditch with her good hand. "He's shutting off the force field."

"Quinn, what happened to your arm?" Jett asked, his smile draining away.

She trembled, and gave a lop-sided smile. "I don't know. The Rekans said this planet turns people to stone. I guess..." she laughed hysterically. "I guess it happened."

She broke down into a mix of hollow laughter and sobs. Jett reached for her, but she pulled away. "Don't touch me! Duke's got it too, so it must spread through touch."

Jett and Robbie exchanged glances. After surviving the terrors they had, being helpless to do anything as their friend was consumed by rock was excruciating. "Perhaps," Robbie said hesitantly, "This is just another one of this planet's tricks?"

"What do you mean?" Jett asked.

"You know, we kept getting smashed, but after the planet transported us somewhere else we'd wake up on a lower level. That seems to be the way of this place. All of this rock is always imploding in on itself."

"Imploding?" Parker repeated. "Do you have any idea of how deranged you sound?" She threw herself against the wall with a moan. "It itches! It hurts and I can't stop it!"

The walls began to grumble, and Jett's adrenaline spiked. Cariss' voice came over the radio. "Your signal is loitering, Robert. You don't have time. Either onward or back, now!"

Jett grabbed Parker's hand and dragged her to the edge of the gap. The memory of clawing at the edge of a chasm flashed through his mind and his heart thumped wildly. "Robbie, your imploding idea is the only chance we've got. One of us needs to catch up with Duke and see if he needs help, the other needs to help Quinn along."

Parker pulled away from him. "Jett, we don't know how this rock-stuff spreads!"

"Go on, Jett," Robbie said. "I'll deal with Quinn."

Giving a quick nod, Jett leaned forward and reached for the rope, and, taking a deep breath, swung across. Robbie turned to Parker. "Come on, Quinn. I'm gonna get you over."

"But now we'll all turn into rock!" she moaned.

He put a strong arm around her and took the dangling rope. "Well, I'm thinking we'll make mighty fine-looking statues." He winked, and taking a few steps back and holding her tightly, he jumped across.

Down the passage, Jett ran around a corner and found himself at a dead end. The cave ended in a rounded room not unlike the one he'd seen earlier. Boxes of equipment littered the ground, and there were several half-built storage shelves. Everything had been left half-finished when the Rekans had realized the planet was dangerous. A large generator was humming, powering several industrial bar lights drilled into the rock ceiling. It also powered a computer perched on a desk.

Duke was pressing the touch-screen in a lame rush, and his eyes were flickering with uncertainty. He jumped up with a start when Jett came in. "Why'd you come here?"

"Aren't you surprised to see me alive?" Jett asked.

Duke hesitated, remembering the glimpse into Parker's future he had seen. "I guessed Cariss might be wrong," he said, hedging around his real reason for not being surprised. "Just because your signal disappears doesn't mean you're dead."

"Do you know what you're doing?" Jett asked, gesturing to the computer.

"It's locked!" he returned. "Where's Robbie?"

"He'll be here in a moment," answered Jett. "He's bringing Parker. Duke, I've got to warn you. The ceilings and the walls come together. Everything gets crushed, and then transported somehow to a lower level in one piece. There are ways to climb up, though. Cariss guided Robbie and me out."

Cariss' voice interrupted from Duke's Hiero. "Duke, Jesse

and Robert are alive and should catch up with you at any moment. Have you reached the controls yet?"

He pulled the radio off his belt. "Yes, and I've got Jett with me too. How do you get into this computer? It's locked!"

"Ivan's looking the passwords up on his device now," she answered. "He doesn't know them, but he thinks they're stored somewhere here in the Communications Center. I'll get back to you as soon as possible."

Footsteps clattered and Robbie appeared, dragging Parker. Jett stepped forward to help him, but Duke stepped forward with a shout. "No!" he cried.

"What?" said Jett.

"Don't touch her. What if this rock spreads through touch?"

Jett shook his head. "I touched her already."

Duke subconsciously fingered his pistol as Jett helped to lay Parker in a corner. Robbie straightened and glanced at Duke. "I can't imagine it spreading by touch, 'cuz how'd Quinn get it in the first place? The Rekans said it happens when the dust gets in your eyes."

Duke searched his memory, trying to pinpoint the moment it had started. He remembered the purple flower he had touched, and how Parker had nearly fallen moments later. It could be related to that, or any number of things on this planet. There was no way of truly knowing or understanding, which made their situation feel all the more precarious and volatile. There was no knowing what would happen or what *could* happen. "We can worry about it later," he said. "But Robbie, I need help. I can't get into this system."

"I can try overriding it," he said, "But after that you'll have to shut down the force field. This is your century, so you'd know their technology best."

Duke stepped back and turned to Jett. "Robbie can hack into anything."

The radio buzzed. "Duke, this is your last shot at the transporter building."

"We've got to shut down the force field!"

Cariss' voice grew stern. "Robert's signal is right beside yours. Send him back immediately. If he can transport back here in time, he can fix the *Starlight*. That would be your only chance out. There is currently no other spacecraft here capable of landing on that surface."

"But will he have enough time to beam over there? Will he have to run through the storm?" asked Jett in concern.

"Depends on how fast he runs," Cariss answered blandly.

"I need time!" Robbie ran his fingers through his hair and then began banging on the desk in agitation. "I can't think of what coding to use. I never hacked into a system like this back in Melville. This is a 23rd century computer... I heard about these things in history but that's it!"

Cariss heard over the radio. "You don't have time, Robert. It's up to you to get the others off that planet."

Jett pushed Robbie aside and began typing. "You don't know anything about code," Robbie shouted, trying to shove his way back. "You're a police officer!"

"I think I know the password." Jett frowned as the computer rejected his attempt, but he began typing again. "Run, Robbie. Get to the transporter!"

Robbie hesitated but then sprinted down the passage. Parker stumbled to her feet. "It hurts!" she cried, tears running down her face. Her words were hardly intelligible. "The rock... won't stop..."

"Calm down, Quinn," Jett called over his shoulder.

Parker's eyes were red and bloodshot. Shaking uncontrollably, she collapsed against the wall. With a sickening crash, her hand shattered, falling to the ground in red, clay-like shards. She screamed.

"Parker!" Jett and Duke shouted in unison, pausing their work at the computer and spinning around.

A tremor ran through the ground, and the two men swayed as they tried to keep their balance. "We can't do anything for her," Jett said, gritting his teeth and turning to the computer. "We've got to shut down that force field."

Duke's eyes were nothing but frigid coals. Without looking at him, Jett knew he was shaking. "How on earth are you going to guess the password?" Duke demanded.

"I'm not guessing," he answered, his attention on the screen. "I know all of Teddy's passwords. I've just got to find the right one."

"He could've come up with new ones in fifteen years," Duke pointed out.

A loud groan blasted through the caverns, shaking like an explosion. Jett staggered and lost his footing, sliding across the room. Duke crashed against the desk. Red, gritty tears covered Parker's face and the room echoed with her scream.

18

The Twins

"Get me outta here, Cariss!" Robbie shouted into his Hiero. After leaving the cave, it had been a struggle for him to reach the shelter of the transporter building. He had been forced to crawl part of the way. The wind was rushing like an airborne jet with the power of a freight train behind it, and even inside the building, he could hear it howling, and the walls quivered beneath it. He shook the sand out of his hair and stared at his Hiero impatiently. "Cariss, are you there?"

Without warning, the transporter was activated, and Robbie was beamed onto the other planet. Cariss was standing there, waiting for him. "Robert," she said immediately, "What's everyone's status?"

"No time! I gotta fix the *Starlight*," he exclaimed, bolting for the door. "I've got to get them off that planet!"

She stepped forward and barred his way, kicking the door shut with her foot. "Quiet," she whispered threateningly. "Listen to me, Robert. I know we don't have any time to spare, but we've got to communicate, or something will go wrong. Keep your voice low; we don't want the whole Center to hear. First of all, I want you to know that Johnson is back in Base."

"Here?" Robbie said with a start.

"Yes. Dr. Emmett and Anton, Johnson's child assistant, if you remember, just brought him back. I want you to fix the *Starlight* and save Duke, but I want you to take Johnson with you."

"With me?" Robbie said, bewildered.

"Shush! We don't know who's side Ivan and the Rekans are truly on," she said. "My personal suspicions are that they are more than happy to let us get them out of their plight, but the moment the force field is down, they will go back to doing things their way. Johnson could easily convince them to follow his lead again, or at least turn them against us. Also, Johnson has time-travelling equipment. It's impossible for him to use it while the force field is active, but the moment Duke shuts it off Johnson can do as he pleases."

Robbie shut his eyes, imagining the chaos that would ensue. Johnson would most likely time-travel out of the picture, and perhaps Ivan and the Rekans would help him. Duke's entire mission was based around putting Johnson on trial for his crimes, and finding Jett's son.

"You must keep him with you at all times," Cariss continued firmly. "Duke and Jett will let me know when they shut the force field off, and I'll pass the information along to you in a coded sentence. I trust you understand why?"

"Because we don't want Johnson to know when the field goes down," Robbie said. "That way, he won't try to escape. I've got to keep him in the dark."

"Exactly," she said. She looked at him sideways. "Robert, I want you to understand how essential this plan is, but I also must warn you of how dangerous it is. Johnson is an extremely smart man. You cannot let him gain control of the situation. Keep your eyes open. This is no longer just about arresting somebody; our lives are on the line. Johnson knows we are here to put a stop to his evildoings, and that will make him desperate. Your life means nothing to him. He tried to steal your ship once, many years ago in his timeline, but not too long ago for you. Don't let him try again."

Robbie swallowed. "Let's pretend everything goes well. I fix the *Starlight*, I fly it over, the force field is down but Johnson doesn't know it, and I've landed on the surface of the Red Planet. What happens next?"

"You've got to get in contact with the others. Duke has ways to disarm Johnson's time-travel equipment, and then we'll escort him to the authorities. That's our end goal."

Robbie nodded, rolling up his sleeves and setting his face in determination. "Got it. When the force field is down, what will the coded message be?"

"'Night is falling on the Red Planet,'" she said. "As that is true, it won't make Johnson suspicious. Now get to work. Perhaps you can convince Dr. Emmett to accompany you. And, Robert..." Her jacket ruffled as she pulled out a gun, pressing it into his hands. "Take this."

He gave a quick nod and then shot out the door. He raced down the Communication Center's hallway; once outside, he slowed down enough to make it down the icy steps without slipping. The wind was strong on this planet as well, but worse, it was dark and snowy. The cold rushed over him, giving his body a shock. Robbie dashed into a quiet street, trying to remember which road would lead him to the Gate.

He spun around when he heard voices. A car was in the street and several people were climbing out. With a surge of excitement, Robbie recognized one of them as Dr. Emmett. He sprinted in that direction, and as he got closer he made out the figures of Johnson, Anton Venedict, and Tate Emmett.

"Robbie!" Dr. Emmett exclaimed as he came up. "Is the force field down?"

In the corner of his eye Robbie noticed Johnson's keen glance. He shook his head. "No. I've got to fix the *Starlight*, and then I'm headed back to see if I can help."

"I know a lot about ship maintenance," Johnson said. "I think I can help you."

"Sure you can," Tate said drily. "You'd fix the thing in no time and then the moment our backs were turned, away you'd go."

"Look here," Johnson said impatiently, "Watch me all you want, but there's not much I can do to mess with your plans now, is there?"

"We've gotta take this chance," Robbie said. "Johnson, you ordered your men to sabotage it. Do you know what they did to it?"

"Of course. I gave them specific instructions, and I should be able to reverse the damage. We've got a warehouse full of spare parts and equipment, and though your ship is far more advanced than anything in this century, we should be able to make do with what we have."

Dr. Emmett grabbed Robbie's shoulder and pulled him aside. "I think Johnson is hoping to get a free ride out of here on your ship," he said in a whisper.

"Course he is, but I'm not gonna let him," Robbie answered. "I don't want him to overhear us, doctor. Let's get to the *Starlight*. We don't have much time."

"Fine, then," Emmett said, "But I'm going to stay with you and keep my eyes open. I'll send Anton and Tate to the Center; Cariss will look after them."

Robbie nodded and then broke away to find the *Starlight* with Johnson in tow. Anton moved to follow them, but Dr. Emmett stopped him by laying a hand on his shoulder.

"Anton, Tate, I want the two of you to wait for us here," he said, kindly but firmly. "I don't want anything to happen to either of you."

Anton and Tate looked at him with identical frowns. "But uncle," Tate protested, "What if something happens to Robbie? What if Jett or Duke have been injured? You guys need a doctor with you!"

Emmett smiled. "I think you're forgetting what I do for a living." More seriously, he continued, "And anyway, Tate, I'm afraid you aren't quite a doctor. If there was a serious injury, I hope you would defer to me or another one of the adults. I appreciate your willingness to help, but I don't want you imagining yourself to be more capable than you are. That can get you into trouble. You've got a lot to learn still: starting with learning to take orders."

Tate folded his arms, his injured pride showing clearly in his eyes. "Whatever you say."

"But I have to come wif you," Anton said anxiously. "Sur Liedr..."

"I want you to stay here," Emmett interrupted firmly. "No buts. You need a bit of a break, son. Tate, keep an eye on him and make sure he sits somewhere and rests."

Dr. Emmett turned to go, but Tate's voice stopped him. "Will everything be all right?"

The young man tried to keep his voice composed and serious, but Dr. Emmett could sense his underlying fear. He looked at them. Tate stood with his arms folded and his feet wide apart, almost in a relaxed position, reminding him strongly of Jett. Anton held his hands clasped behind his back and he was leaning forwards slightly, poised like an arrow set to string. That was how Emmett remembered Maddie. She and Jett were always ready, but she let it show more than him.

"I don't know," Emmett said, answering Tate's question. "I'm sorry, boys. Stay together and stay safe."

He gave them one final glance. They were Jett and Maddie's sons, that was for sure, paradox or no. Dr. Emmett had loved and cared for both of them since the moment he saw them: Tate, as a baby, and Anton, only hours earlier. He had never imagined that they were both his blood relatives, born in his own hometown of Angel. But he was convinced it was true, no matter how impossible. Knowing that they were Jett's sons strengthened his resolve to keep them safe and take them away from all this chaos and bring them home, back to Angel, where they belonged.

19

Nightfall

"Hurry!" Duke shouted, grabbing the side of the desk and pulling himself onto his knees. The ground was quaking and dust rose up like clouds of smoke. Jett steadied himself against the desk and blinked red flecks out of his eyes.

Squinting, he tried to make sense of the shaking screen. The constant tossing of the room was causing his stomach to rise. Swallowing it down, he pressed a line of digits and held his breath. At last, the password was accepted and the login screen disappeared.

"It worked!" Duke exclaimed, reaching over and pressing buttons. Jett sank back, taking a deep breath. He scooted over to where Parker lay, and carefully he helped her sit up. The cavern was still shaking, and the rock was still groaning, but in his own mind, everything became still and quiet. He had done what was needed of him; he was no longer under any pressure and there was nothing more he could do. His surroundings slipped into his subconscious and he let himself focus only on the people in the room.

"We'll get through this," he whispered.

"My heart is rock," Parker said dully. "I shouldn't be alive."

"I've learned today that we can live through some pretty crazy things," said Jett. "We'll get you out of here."

"Thanks," she said. Her voice was lifeless, and her eyes were fixed dead ahead. "Jett, I can't see." Her eyes were red stone. Jett watched as her eyelids closed and stuck fast, and her head dropped against his shoulder.

Duke came crawling over, staying on his hands and knees to keep his balance amid the shaking. "Are you done?" Jett asked, leaning against the rock wall.

Duke nodded. "The force field is down."

He sat on the other side of Jett. Wearily he lifted his Hiero. "It's done, Cariss. We're going to let ourselves get swallowed by the rock once, to see if it revives Parker. Standby to help us out."

The rock rumbled, but to Jett it was a distant sound. "I wish it would swallow us already," he said quietly. Parker's head felt heavy on his shoulder. "I don't like the wait."

"Jett, I'm sorry," Duke gushed, turning into the apologetic man Jett had first met on his doorstep back in Nebraska. "I guilted you into coming. I knew this would be dangerous work, time-travel always is, but I swear I never imagined all of this would happen."

"Sure, I was guilted in," Jett said. "But it's my duty to find my son, isn't it? Do you think Teddy has him on the other planet?"

"Yes, your son is there," Duke said. "I felt the time-displacement, but I'm afraid I was too occupied to actually see where it was coming from. I felt your son's presence, I guess is what I'm trying to say."

"What else can you do?" asked Jett, truly curious. "Dr. Emmett said something about you being able to read people's minds."

"I can, sometimes," Duke said listlessly. "Thoughts and memories seem to tie into time somehow. I feel it all and I can travel through it all. Your son, Tate: you know how he can sense what his twin is thinking and feeling?"

Jett nodded.

"Your twins were formed in a paradox. They're children of time. They have a strong connection to each other because of that, but I wouldn't be surprised if they could telepathically pick up thoughts and memories from other people as well. For myself, I think I'm a touch telepath."

"That must be convenient," Jett said.

"No, it isn't!" Duke said. The fire in his eyes dwindled into cold coals. "I never asked for this power, Jett, and I never would. It kills me, it rips me apart."

"But can't you control it?" Jett asked, growing concerned for his own sons.

Duke's eyes darkened as he remembered the wedding he had slipped into earlier. "No, I can't. What can I do with it? It's something beyond what you can understand, Jett, and it's killed me. I used to be the most oblivious man on earth, and I was the happiest. But now, I'm randomly thrown into different time periods. I've been forced to watch my own future and my past. And with an accidental touch, I'm exposed to all the feelings of everyone around me."

Jett felt a rush of heat against his wrist. Glancing down, he saw Duke's hand touching his arm, enclosed in a transparent flame. Jett dimly realized that his friend was telepathically listening to his thoughts. In a slurred voice, Duke spoke.

"Jesse King, for a quiet man, your feelings are strong. You've got fear, resignation, and shame... what's that from, I wonder? But mostly you're afraid. Forefront on your mind are memories of your son Logan by the fishing hole, and Teddy is holding his hand. But now you're mixing your memories. I see a ragged man trapped underground, Parker's eyes are closing, children are dying of starvation..."

"Stop!" Jett yelled, tearing himself away.

Duke was quivering. "I'm sorry, Jett. But do you understand? No man should have this power, for his sake and the sake of others."

"What *happened* to you?" Jett demanded. "Why are you able to do that?"

Duke hesitated. "You wouldn't believe me. Nobody does. But I'm worried that Tate and his twin might find themselves capable of everything I can do. I hope not, but it could happen."

Before Jett could respond, the passage roared and the walls swung out. This time there was no ignoring it. Jett felt the familiar surge of adrenaline, but he forced himself to stay still, gripping Parker's still form. As the ceiling fell, the last thing he saw was Duke looking at him, his eyes burning with regret that he didn't understand.

Meanwhile, the *Starlight* took off from Reka II. Johnson had proven to be a capable genius, and the ship had been repaired. It hadn't been a difficult fix, just a rerouting of some wires, but without knowing what was wrong, it would have taken Robbie a while to find the problem. Using both warp speed and the field displacer, the ship entered the red planet's orbit in a matter of seconds.

Carefully Robbie lowered the *Starlight* into the atmosphere, and they immediately encountered intense wind. The lower they dropped, the more fierce the weather grew.

"Cariss, where's their signal?" Robbie asked the radio.

"You're almost directly above it," she answered. "I'm trying to contact them but they won't respond. I believe they will need my help guiding them out of the caverns soon. Careful, Robert. Night is falling on that planet."

Robbie gripped his controls and nodded, remembering what the coded message meant. "Yeah, it's getting darker. But worse, this wind is strong."

"The *Starlight* is meant for space," she said. "Its features and engines for flying in an air-filled atmosphere are limited."

Dr. Emmett nodded. "Is there something you can do, Robbie? This ship is shaking like crazy."

"Oh, I hadn't noticed," Robbie said drily. "But seriously, the *Starlight* doesn't know what to do with wind. Heavens, she's not a helicopter. Cariss, I can't land in this."

"Evaluate the situation and fly out if need be," Cariss answered. "I have to go, Robert. Duke's on the other line."

The radio went quiet. Johnson was hovering behind Robbie's chair, watching his movements and listening to the conversation. "The storm will pass by soon," he said, "then you'll be able to land."

Robbie shrugged. "We can only hope. You might want to

sit down; there's going to be a lot of rough spots. My ship barely knows what to do with gravity, let alone wind storms."

Something cold and metal pressed against the back of Robbie's head. "I'm giving orders now," Johnson said quietly.

Dr. Emmett took a step forward, but Johnson lifted the pistol in his hand, covering both of them. Robbie glared. "I'd like to know how you got that."

"You had it in your pocket. Ask Jesse; he knows I've always been an expert at sleight-of-hand deals," he answered. He sent a menacing look towards the doctor. "Stay still! As for you, Captain Robert, I want you to land this thing. I want you to unlock the force field."

Robbie's eyes widened. "But... don't you know? Duke and Jett... are trying to!"

"Duke and Jesse will die. No one survives that planet."

"What makes you think we've got a better chance?"

Johnson wavered. "Perhaps we don't. But I can't let Reka die."

20

Johnson's Watch

Red sand rushed across the viewing screens. Robbie eyed one of the control gauges that told him their elevation; they were quickly dropping. The wind tugged on the *Starlight* and he nearly lost his seat. Johnson still stood behind the pilot's chair, his pistol in his hand, and his feet set wide apart as an anchor against the tossing of the ship.

Cariss' voice crackled over the radio. "Robert, give me an update."

"Ignore her," Johnson ordered.

"Don't have the concentration to answer her anyway," Robbie snapped. He sighed, mentally berating himself. "She warned me," he muttered.

Johnson pressed his weapon against his head. "What was that?"

"Nothing!"

"Tell me!"

"Cariss warned me about you, that's all. Now let me land my ship."

A sneer full of sick satisfaction crossed Johnson's face.

"Ha!" he said, "I guess you didn't take the warning seriously. Or maybe it's the fact that you're nothing against me. You're just a pilot, and barely that."

Robbie was seething. His mind was busy trying to think of ways to get out of his predicament. Unbeknownst to Johnson, the force field was already off. But if Johnson knew, there was nothing to keep him from time-travelling away. Robbie clenched his teeth and mentally berated himself for letting Johnson gain control so easily. Cariss had warned him. He knew he should attempt to disarm him, but the thought terrified him. Robbie wasn't a fighter. Like Johnson said, he was a pilot. Suddenly, an idea came to his mind.

He would use gravity to his advantage. The *Starlight* had artificial gravity, which kept their feet to the ground when they were in space. Glancing at the control panel, he noticed with satisfaction that it was still active. It was the only reason they weren't sliding across the floor in all the wind. Slowly, he tilted the ship onto its side. Johnson and Dr. Emmett didn't notice the change, as the artificial gravity kept them upright.

Robbie pressed his feet against the ground and flipped off the artificial gravity. Instantly, Dr. Emmett was flung from his seat. Johnson slid off his feet and slammed into the panels. In a flash, Robbie abandoned the controls and wrenched the pistol from his hand. Hiero radios, papers, tools and anything that wasn't fastened down was being thrown back and forth as the craft spiralled out of control. Johnson struggled to regain his footing, but Robbie rammed him against the control panel and then pushed him away.

"Keep him down, doc," Robbie shouted, shoving the pistol

into his belt and sliding into the pilot seat. He quickly righted the ship's course and turned the artificial gravity back on, and the tossing inside ceased.

"You must think you're so smart, boy," Johnson said, clutching his side and staggering to his feet. Dr. Emmett eyed him warily. "I suppose that now you've outsmarted me, you're going to fly back to Base."

"I've come too far to turn back now," Robbie answered. "And I don't think I'm exceptionally smart, but I want you to know I'm the pilot of this ship and I give the orders."

"Robert, are you there? Answer me!" the radio crackled.

He grabbed the Hiero. "I'm trying to land, Cariss. Wait a moment!"

"I thought you couldn't land in that weather!"

"We had a slight episode with Johnson that brought me very close to a flat place to land, so I'm gonna go for it."

He tossed the Hiero aside. Behind him, Johnson glared. Rage and vengeance showed clearly on his face, and, Dr. Emmett imagined, envy. The *Starlight* was an amazing ship, and Johnson had once imagined that it would be his.

"I can do this," Robbie muttered to himself. With a final swoop, he propelled the *Starlight* into the high mesa where Duke and Parker had entered the cavern earlier. The ship struck and spasmed, and Robbie cut the engine.

"I did it," he said, surprise showing clearly on his face. A moment later it was chased away by delight. He jumped to his feet, grabbing the radio. "My landing gear will never be the same again," he exclaimed, "But I did it!"

There was a sharp, buzzing noise. "Doesn't that mean

someone is trying to get in?" Dr. Emmett asked. Robbie stood and touched the wall and the invisible door slid open.

There stood Duke. His clothes and hair were ruffled and filled with red sand, and his hands were scraped, but he was alive. "Robbie!" he said immediately. "You're going to wreck this thing!"

"Where are Jett and Parker? Are they all right?" Robbie asked, jumping out of the *Starlight*.

"We're right here," Jett answered, coming up. "It worked, Robbie. It was just another one of the planet's tricks. After getting swallowed, when we woke up, Parker was back to normal. I don't know whether this planet just made an illusion of her turning into stone, or if it's some kind of physics that we don't understand, but she's not rock anymore."

Parker stood beside him, with her lopsided smile and shining eyes. Jett was right. Though he didn't understand it, Robbie could see that Parker was no longer stone, but living and breathing. Something caught in his throat, and he and Parker met with a hug. After releasing her, he grasped Jett's hand and shook it violently. "I've brought Dr. Emmett," he said, "And Johnson."

As if on cue, Johnson staggered up to the door. His eyes were heavy and haunted, and he gripped the door with un-usual strength. "Duke, Jesse," he greeted with a slight nod. He paused, and then spoke again quietly. "The force field is down, isn't it?"

Jett nodded.

Slowly, Johnson stepped out of the ship and began to walk

a few paces away. Robbie and Dr. Emmett glanced at Duke in concern.

"Where are you going?" asked Duke.

None of them made any movement to follow him. Jett called, "Teddy, we need to talk."

"I don't want to talk," Johnson answered, stopping. His hand went to his wrist.

Duke stepped forward. "Johnson, I'm afraid I must escort you back to earth to face a trial with the Space Agency."

Johnson turned to face them. "Well, what are you waiting for?"

Duke held out his hand. "Let me see your watch."

Slowly, Johnson lifted his arm. He pulled up his coat sleeve, and to everyone's surprise and consternation, there was nothing on his wrist. His near manic laugh echoed through the mountains. "I don't have it! I couldn't time-travel if I wanted to! My watch is safe, and you will never find it, Duke! You will not have your petty revenge on me for meddling with time. What makes you think time belongs to you anyway?" He laughed again.

Duke shook his head. "All of us are given our own time, Johnson, plenty of it, and that should satisfy us. I must ask you to come with me."

"But what about Reka? They need my help to recover. How about a deal? You want your son back, don't you, Jesse? Well, I'll give him back if you give me a second chance."

"Don't try to make deals with me," Jett said. His heart was thumping wildly. His voice broke as he tried to speak again. "You can't barter my son to save yourself from a life in prison; you've got to reap what you sow. I thought you were my friend, Teddy. If you won't help me find my child, I'll find him myself."

"I found him," Dr. Emmett said softly. "Do you remember Anton Venedict?"

Johnson balled his fists. "Well, he's all yours, Jesse King. You're calling me out on being a wretched friend, but I know a few things about you. You don't even care about your sons. The day I took the baby, he was crying and you didn't care because Maddie was dying and you were too angry to face him. That's the only reason the paradox happened in the first place! I took Anton and Tate because I knew you could never care!"

Jett felt a lump grow in his throat. Teddy had told him about what had happened the day the paradox had taken place. The memory burned in his mind, the scalding memory he had tried so hard to forget. Maddie was on the easy-chair, laboring to even breathe. Familiar anger overwhelmed him. Maddie didn't deserve this, she deserved to live. Logan, only a toddler, was breaking his crayons because he wanted attention. And from the other room, Jett could hear the baby crying, but he didn't care. He was too angry to care.

He stood there, staggered by the shame he had never confessed, not even to himself. Dr. Emmett took up the conversation for him. "Johnson, you gave Tate the life of an orphan. You've hurt Anton in more ways than the boy is willing to admit. I'm guessing it would've been better if you had left them with Jett!"

The wind hurled Johnson's bitter laugh towards them with a rush of red sand. "How could I have known what I would turn into? Yes, I've hurt Anton, more times that I let myself remember. But he's all I've got to live for. If you have any compassion, don't take him from me!"

"You kidnapped him," Dr. Emmett said.

"It was for him!" Johnson shrieked. "Jett wouldn't have loved his sons and he never will!"

"Stop!" Jett shouted. His voice was raw with emotion. "Stop! I know I didn't care. You would never have been able to take my sons if it hadn't been for my own indifference. I haven't done my duty to them, I haven't spent time with them, protected them, or loved them, and I regret it more than I'll ever regret anything. It will hurt me, it will hurt you, and I know it'll hurt Anton, but I'm going to fix things. My indifference ends here, Johnson."

"So it's 'Johnson' now, no more 'Teddy'? Don't destroy my life, I beg you. Leave me with Anton on Reka."

"You aren't Teddy," Jett said, his heart breaking with every word. "You're a cruel, cowardly liar."

Johnson's maniacal look died away. "Success will turn anyone into a coward," he said. "It gives you much more to lose."

"Your success with Reka and time-travel ends here, I'm afraid," Duke said. "If the *Kenswick* has the security for it, I'll ask them to escort you back to Earth, as a prisoner."

Parker touched Duke's arm. "What about Anton? What will happen to him?"

"Put him on the *Kenswick*," Dr. Emmett suggested. "The trip back to Earth is three months, right? We can meet them there after Anton has had some time to say goodbye."

"I'll certainly speak to the captain of the *Kenswick*," Duke decided. "Robbie, take us back to Reka II."

21

Conclusion

That night, bunk beds were provided in the back room of the Communications Center for Jett, Robbie, Parker, Tate, and Dr. Emmett. Jett wasn't sure if Duke or Cariss slept or not; it seemed like they spent the whole night making sure Johnson was put in a cell for safe-keeping, talking with the *Kenswick's* captain, and sorting out the food distribution with Ivan. When morning came, everything was settled. The Rekans had begun the work of saving the survivors with food and medical attention, and the *Kenswick's* Captain was thoroughly prepared to take Johnson to Earth as a criminal and Anton as a passenger.

When Jett woke up, his head was aching and his mind was groggy with confusion. He hadn't the slightest idea of what time it was (or what time it would be for him if he was relative to the right century) and he barely knew where he was. Robbie was still sleeping in the bunk above him. Jett got up, attempted to smooth his hair in the bathroom mirror, and then pulled on his North Face jacket, before making his way outside.

Standing on the front steps of the Communication Center, he surveyed the morning view. The sun was rising, coloring the mountain snow with rays of yellow and orange. Millions of stars still blazed in the sky, shining brilliantly enough that even the planet's sun couldn't overpower them. The cold air nipped at his skin, and he pulled his jacket a little tighter. Even as early as sunrise, there was activity going on there in Base. Workers were stocking the warehouses, while cars glided in and out of the Gate with food and medicine for the distant towns.

"'Morning, Jesse," Dr. Emmett greeted, coming up behind him. "It's quite a view, isn't it?"

Jett nodded. "Sunrise on Reka is something I won't forget in a long while."

Dr. Emmett sat down on the concrete step and folded his hands over his knees. "So, Jett, how are you doing?"

Jett sighed and sat down beside him. "As well as can be expected, I suppose. You know, Doctor, I really thought for a moment that I was going to die on that Red Planet. I thought of how Logan would never know what happened to me. I wonder what Maddie would think of everything I did yesterday."

Dr. Emmett laid a hand on his shoulder. "Jett, you handled yourself very well. I'm impressed with how you managed every situation that came up. Things are going to be very different, now that you have two new sons who are a lot older than they should be. I want you to know that I'm going to help as much as I can."

Jett winced. "Could you start with telling me exactly what to do? I'll do anything to fix my family, no matter how hard, but the thing is I'm completely lost. My best friend is gone, so I can't confide in him anymore..." He trailed off, and then began again. "What am I supposed to do with Anton? I want to take him home, of course, but what if that isn't right? He's lived his whole life in this century, so perhaps it would be easier on him if the people here did something. He must be close to someone besides Johnson. Maybe some Rekan family wants him to live with them, or maybe an Agency on earth will put him in some sort of program."

Emmett shook his head. "You've got to take him home with you. From a medical standpoint, I believe Anton has experienced enough trauma here that he won't want to stay unless he's with Johnson, which isn't an option."

"But I can't just drag him to Nebraska. I'm a stranger to him. I know I'm his father, but does that give me the right to drag him wherever I want?"

"No, no. Sit down and talk with him like a father to son, or an older brother to a younger, if that makes you more comfortable. If you leave him here, you're putting him in someone else's power: Johnson's, or whatever people there are in the 23rd century who would love to conform Anton to their own agenda. I don't want you to assert power over him. That's Johnson's way. I'm telling you to take responsibility."

Jett nodded, and his features steeled in determination. "I'll do it. I'll do whatever I can for him and Tate. And Logan."

Dr. Emmett smiled. "I know you will, Jesse. Now, I don't mean to hurt you in any way, but have you ever considered remarrying?"

Jett's face fell. "Of course. Maddie told me to before she

died. It doesn't hurt me to talk about it, doctor, so feel free to say what you're thinking."

"Parker's a brave, pretty girl," the doctor said. "I bet she'd love to meet Logan."

Jett ran his fingers through his hair thoughtfully, right as Duke came up. "Good morning," he greeted, sitting beside them. "Whenever the others wake up, we can board the *Starlight* and fly out of here. We'll use time-travel to skip over two months to when Johnson and Anton are arriving on Earth. After that, I'll take you back to 21st century Nebraska."

"Will you take us back to the exact time that we left? As if we'd never left at all?" Jett asked.

"I can, if you want me to."

Jett shook his head. "To me, Duke, it feels as if I've been gone from home for a day and a half. And even in the 23rd century I've aged a day and a half, haven't I? When I go back home, I want it to be that much time later: a day and a half, for example. Do you see what I mean?"

Duke nodded. "If you spend a day running around Reka I, you're a day older. If I brought you back to the moment you left, around 2 o'clock, Saturday, you'd be too old, technically. You want me to bring you back on Sunday, or Monday, or however many days later we spend here in the 23rd century."

"You can do that, can't you? Just keep track of how long we've been gone, and take us back that much later. I don't want Logan to ever see me older than I should be, like I saw Johnson." He shuddered.

"I'll make sure that doesn't happen," Duke agreed.

"I wonder," Jett said, his mind wandering, "if Teddy Johnson would have done everything he did if I had time-travelled with him when he asked me to. He's always been impulsive, and of course he makes mistakes, but I used to always save him in the nick of time."

"True, but you've got to understand that that's what Johnson was running from," Dr. Emmett said. "He didn't want accountability. Be thankful you have accountability, son. We all need it."

Cariss Swusterlinn stepped out of the Center's doors. "Good morning, Dr. Emmett, good morning, Jesse."

"Good morning," Jett said, as he and the doctor stood up. "I meant to tell you this yesterday, but I didn't get the chance. Thanks for helping us over the radio. You saved our lives."

"You're welcome," she said, as blandly as she said everything. "I hope you slept well?"

"Yes, I did."

"Good. Duke, we can leave whenever you're ready."

"Whenever our pilot wakes up," Duke said.

"He's awake," she informed him. "They're all awake and should be out here any minute."

The door opened and Parker stepped out. Her blond hair was falling out of her bun and her eyelids were drooping. "Hey, everyone," she greeted, smiling her lopsided smile. "Sorry I slept in."

"Don't worry," Duke started, right as Jett started to speak. He took an imperceptible step back and went silent, letting Jett take up the conversation.

"Not a problem, Parker," he said. "We're still waiting for Robbie. Does anyone know where Anton is? I'd like to say goodbye to him."

"Duke and I told him about how Johnson was going on trial, and how he will be going to his family in Nebraska," Cariss said. "Personally, I would advise you against saying anything to him right now. He did not appreciate the news."

Tate and Robbie stepped out. "Are we heading out now?" the latter asked with a yawn.

"That's the plan," said Duke.

"Can y'all believe it?" Parker said, stepping between Duke and Jett. She gazed at the Rekan sunrise with shining eyes. "We saved this colony, didn't we? All of those people out there will survive now."

"They owe everything to you, Parker," Dr. Emmett said. "You, Jett, Robbie, Duke and Cariss. We came out here to catch Johnson, but we did a lot more than just that."

A troubled expression crossed Jett's face. "Johnson's watch is still out there somewhere. Whoever finds it will be able to time-travel."

"I'll find it," Duke promised. "I have quite a few loose ends to tie up."

Slowly, they made their way out of Base. Snow crunched beneath their feet, and a slight wind edged with ice made them shiver. Several crewmen of the *Kenswick* waved as they walked past, and even a few Rekans did a traditional bow and touch of the forehead. The Gate was wide open, and they walked through and out into the frozen wasteland. There they had a final view of the mountains in all their lofty splendor, and the glittering, frozen lake.

They turned their backs on the cold beauty around them and boarded the *Starlight*. Robbie and Cariss sat at the controls, while Duke and Dr. Emmett sat in the extra two seats next to them. Jett, Parker and Tate took their places on the seats against the back wall.

The viewing screens powered on and the engine hummed into life. "Duke, open the channel to the Communications Center," Robbie said.

Duke quickly did so. "This is Captain Robert Juno Finley of the *Starlight 3000*," Robbie announced over the radio. "Requesting permission for takeoff."

"Permission granted," Ivan's voice answered.

"This is the Captain of the *Kenswick*," a new voice joined in. "Safe travels, and thank you for all of your help. I'll be bringing Johnson back to Earth shortly. See you there."

"Is Anton with you?" Jett asked, half-rising from his seat.

"No," Ivan's voice answered, "he is not. He has locked himself in an empty storeroom and refuses to come out."

Jett sank back into his chair. "Tell him I said goodbye."

"I will do zat."

Duke shut off the channel and Robbie prepared for takeoff. Quickly and smoothly, the *Starlight* glided out of the landing field and over Base, over the mountain, and over Johnson's cabin. Jett only realized he was staring at the floor vacantly when Parker laid a hand on his shoulder.

"It'll be all right," she assured him. "Trust me, it will."

Up front, Duke gazed at the glassy control panel that, like a mirror, reflected a blurred image of Parker and Jett. His mind clouded with a dark memory. His heart aching with regret, he watched the reflection of a future that could never be.

THE END

Notes

What about the wedding? Does Jett die? Will Anton ever accept the changes in his life? What are Ivan's plans, and are things over for Johnson? Who has Johnson's watch?

Obviously this isn't the end of the story! Actually, *Alchemist of Eternity* is just the beginning. This book is the first in the *Paradox* Series, which follows the adventures of eight main characters: Jett King, Robbie Finley, Parker Quinn, Duke, Dr. Emmett, Cariss, and the twins, Anton and Tate.

Characters in order of appearance:

Teddy R. **Johnson** (*Sur Liedr* or president of Reka; former best friend of Jett)

Anton Venedict (paradox twin)

Ivan Koswitch (*Sil Liedr* or vice president of Reka)

Jesse (**Jett**) King (main character; a police officer from Angel, NE)

Janet Mitchell (the babysitter)

Logan King (Jett and Maddie's six-year-old son)

Maddie King (Jett's deceased wife)

Duke (time-traveller from 23rd century with a mission to arrest Johnson)

Parker Quinn (Duke's assistant)

Dr. Ronald **Emmett** (relative of Jett; doctor from Angel, NE)

Robert (**Robbie**) Juno Finley (Duke's assistant; from the future; captain of the *Starlight*)

Thomas (**Tate**) Emmett (paradox twin)

Dr. **Cariss** Swusterlinn (psychiatrist in Angel, NE; friend of Duke's)